Sin for Breakfast

MASON HOFFENBERG

Sin for Breakfast

GRAFTON BOOKS
A Division of the Collins Publishing Group

LONDON GLASGOW
TORONTO SYDNEY AUCKLAND

Grafton Books
A Division of the Collins Publishing Group
8 Grafton Street, London W1X 3LA

Published by Grafton Books 1989

First published in Great Britain by
The Olympia Press Ltd 1967

Copyright © Mason Hoffenberg 1967
            Zéline Guéna 1989

ISBN 0-586-20195-5

Printed and bound in Great Britain by
Collins, Glasgow

Set in Times

1

If anyone in the café thought it odd that he had been sitting for over half an hour without shifting his gaze from the house across the street he hardly cared. There was a magnificent view of Oliver's door and that was all that mattered. Occasionally a car drove up the street, and, for an instant, the door would be obscured behind it. When this happened he would sharpen his attention so that the instant seemed to take a perilously long time. As soon as the car had passed and the door was visible again Trent's eyes fixed hungrily on it as if, in the next second, it might open and somebody step out.

When he'd finished his second coffee, he got up, put a hundred-franc note under the saucer, and crossed the street.

Inside the house it was cool and silent. He tiptoed up the stairs and stood outside Oliver's room, his ear to the door and trembling slightly. There was no sound. He pictured him in there, lying curled up in the bed, alone, probably, and with some book he'd been reading and his cigarettes lying on the floor beside the bed. He'd probably gone to sleep about three o'clock and was going to wake up at noon. That would give him another two hours. Perhaps he'd stayed out all night and wasn't there at all for that matter. He considered opening the door – his own key would work he'd discovered one time when Oliver had been locked out – but a wave of embarrassment overcame him. If, by chance, Oliver were awake and lying in bed reading, or smoking a cigarette, it would be too ridiculous for him to enter like that and be caught in all the dense silliness of his suspicion.

He turned and went back down the stairs making as little sound as possible. Once in the street, however, he regretted his lack of nerve. One glance at the room, empty, or with Oliver in it alone, would have freed him, but, as things stood, he was a prisoner to the vicinity until he'd made certain that just this was the case, that, for example, nobody else was there. By 'nobody else' he meant Vivian.

He went back to the café again and ordered another coffee. After a while he bought a newspaper and pretended to be reading it but his gaze remained on Oliver's door and, in his mind, for the hundredth time he went over what had happened that morning to cause him to be sitting there.

It was because of the abruptness with which she'd gotten out of bed that he'd woken up; there had been something hurried and deliberate in the way she'd done it, as if something were up. He remembered asking her sleepily where she was going and that she had answered that she was going shopping at the Bon Marché. After that he'd made believe he'd gone back to sleep – covering his face with his hand and watching her through the cracks between his fingers. That was something he often did in the mornings. He liked to watch her dress and to pretend that she was a woman he didn't know and that he was peeping at her through a keyhole. It was also the only way that he could get a look at her body at such moments, for she was inordinately shy and would have managed to conceal her nudity if she suspected he was watching. Not that there was anything for her to be ashamed of, he had thought, as she'd sat in the chair, one of her shapely legs

6

raised in the air, and slowly pulled the long silk stocking on. No, on the contrary, any other woman, if she were that good-looking, would take every opportunity to parade about naked in front of her husband and let the rest of the men see a few things too – lean over innocently while seated in a café, for example, and let them see that those were really her breasts that swelled out like that, and not the rubber form of some trick brassiere; or sit on a sofa the way some women did, with her legs curled up beneath her so that any man who happened to be opposite could see everything she had whenever she changed her position. In a way, he was sorry she wasn't like those other women; it would have been exciting if, once in a while, she would deliberately do something shocking – take his hand and suddenly rub it between her legs, or, when she was going up a flight of stairs ahead of him, yank her skirt up unexpectedly and show him her bottom . . . It was better she didn't, of course. He didn't really have much time for that sort of thing, and if their lovemaking was a bit perfunctory and not very frequent it was all to the good. He had begun to think about his thesis and about his work at the School of Oriental Languages and then it had happened.

She had been standing, fully clothed by now; in the black velvet dress which went so perfectly with her blonde hair; and dabbing herself about the face and neck with the perfume he'd given her for her birthday, when suddenly she raised her skirt and rested her foot on a chair. She had her back to him, and he remembered looking at the foot on the chair, in its high-heeled patent-leather pump, wondering what she was doing before discovering that it was all being reflected in the full-length mirror on the closet door.

To his astonishment, he noticed, first: that she had neglected to put on her panties and that, for once, he was afforded an excellent view of the furry spot between her legs, and, even more extraordinary, that she was touching herself there with her index finger. He realized that for some incredible reason she was perfuming this secret part of her anatomy. It was really unbelievable. He'd been with her for two years now and had never seen anything like it. Before it was over she had actually spread the lips of her sex apart with two fingers and dabbed some of the scent between them. He had all he could do to keep still in the bed and continue the farce of being asleep. A minute later and she had swept out of the room and he heard the front door open and shut very quietly.

He had sprung out of the bed then, and, pulling on his bathrobe, had dashed into the kitchen whose window gave on to the street. Standing there, hidden behind a curtain, he had observed yet another inexplicable thing: instead of crossing the avenue to where the bus stopped that went to Sevres-Babylone and the department store, she was remaining on their side as if she were going to take a bus in the other direction.

'Oliver,' he had thought. There could be no other explanation, that was absolutely the only time they ever took the ninety-one bus going that way. But what the hell was she going to Oliver's for at nine o'clock in the morning? All of this unusual behavior of hers, offered up as soon as he awoke, was going to take a few minutes to comprehend. The solution, however, wasn't very complicated. If a woman gets up, puts a bit of perfume on her pussy, and then takes the bus to your best friend's house, it doesn't look like she's going shopping. But Oliver! Good old chubby Oliver! This was something he'd have to see to believe.

He stayed at the window long enough to watch her board the bus and then, with his heart beating fast, hurriedly dressed and washed and was, himself, mounting a ninety-one bus eight minutes later.

Once arrived, however, he had had a wave of doubt. Should he just go storming right into the room like a maniac? After all, maybe she wasn't even there. Maybe she had some lover that he didn't know about that lived in the same *quartier* as Oliver. Or maybe she was visiting Oliver but it wasn't what he thought – she might just be in there talking about something, but about what? About how pretty her pussy smelled and wouldn't Oliver maybe like to have a sniff? It was incredible. He decided to have a cup of coffee at the corner café where he could watch the door of the house and consider the situation.

That had been an hour ago. During that time his belief in Vivian's culpability had dwindled considerably. Now that he had gone and listened outside the door, and heard nothing, he was almost ready to give the whole thing up for a wild suspicion. He was starting to get an ache in his neck besides, from not having moved his head for all that time. All right, he thought, I'll give it one more try and if I don't hear anything I'll go back home. She would probably say something that night that would clear the whole thing up without his even asking . . .

Only this time he *did* hear something. It was so loud that he hadn't even gotten to the door and heard it as soon as he started up the stairs. It was unmistakable – the sound of a bed taking a beating, the springs creaking steadily up and down.

The key didn't make a sound. He pushed the door open and there it was – Oliver's big white ass pumping away for dear life. It looked like a frantic washerwoman kneeling over a tub of dirty clothes, and, underneath, the

9

laundry being pummeled was Vivian all right. A glance at the white legs, dangling and kicking lasciviously in the air was enough. There was no need to see the face, contorted, as if in pain and with the tongue avidly licking the mouth of her lover.

For what seemed like a long time he stood watching in shocked disbelief as Oliver's shivering buttocks rose and crashed down, driving stiffly into Vivian; knocking the breath out of her, so that each downward plunge was accompanied by her gasp – and then the door clicked shut behind him.

Instantly, the activity on the bed came to a halt. The silence was absolute in the room and faintly, as if from very far away, he heard the screeching scooters and the snarling trucks of the Paris morning.

The two faces staring at him were expressionless and it was he, as he took the pistol from his back pocket and pointed it to his temple, who wore a foolish and embarrassed grin, as if he had stumbled into the room by mistake.

Several times, and rapidly, he squeezed on the trigger and the little jets of water splattered hard against his forehead and trickled ludicrously down, wetting his shirt.

Then he turned and left, being very careful not to slam the door.

2

Trent hummed a Christmas carol. He was already several blocks from Oliver's house, striding along in a brisk, determined way, and, in his head, a choir of little children was singing . . . 'Love and Joy come to you, and to you your Wassail true . . .'; over and over, and in tones of purest crystal, they sang the silly rhyme and Larry hummed in accompaniment.

A wall, a marvelous wall of delight encompassed him. A wall, on the other side of which, and safely locked out, stood the monotonous and plodding existence which had been his life. He patrolled the wall in joyous admiration of its height, its thickness, and its utter lack of entrances. Inside was the Garden of Freedom, the Park of Nascent Possibilities, replete with Love and Joy and complimentary formulas.

There was nothing, he reflected, to prevent him from marching straight to the Champs-Elysées and buying a shiny new Jaguar, nothing to stop him from getting into it and driving right off to Cannes, or Rappalo, or Malaga. He could start a brand-new life – anything at all. He need never give another thought to his wife or to the two hundred and fourteen radicals of the Chinese language, or to the eight hundred and eighty-eight phonetics of same, or to his widowed mother, or to his dead father, or to 'good old chubby Oliver', or the concierge, or their goddamned Siamese cat that was always pissing on the sofa. Neither did he have to worry about his eighteen thousand dollars worth of stocks and bonds – except how best to spend them for his own completely selfish pleasure. It was over; in one gorgeous stroke the past had been locked out.

Flying would be even better he thought, ticking off the fantastic possibilities, you could go faster and further. He might decide to do *that* when he got to the Champs-Elysées – that was where all the airlines had their offices and their windows full of posters depicting far-away wonderful places. It should be possible, with a careful itinerary, to spend your life constantly attending great national holidays – carnival-time in Rio, and afterwards you hop a plane for Marrakesh in time for the Ramadan where, for a month, you spend each day fasting (and sleeping to make it easier), and pass each tropic night eating your guts off and carousing. Then there was Vernal Equinox day in Foochow, when the whole city went insane; May Day in Moscow, Derby Day in Derby, Mahatma Ghandi Day in Benares, Christmas in Dublin and New Year's in New York. As for Paris, aside from the eve of Bastille Day, he wouldn't ever have any call to be there again.

He would arrive on the scene in appropriate costume and with his suitcase crammed full of funny hats and pennants, of cow-bells, and whiskey and Hallowe'en candy; of tennis-balls, scumbags, mistletoe, castanets, Easter eggs, field-glasses, confetti, thuribles and fire-crackers. He might have a few anthropology books also, and pass away the time on the plane boning up on the deeper significance of the festivities he was about to attend.

And what about women? He realized with a cold certainty what a huge and unassuaged yen had lain lurking in him all those years of continence. He would make a hell of a Romeo with all that money. He could have all

12

sorts of women: fifteen-year-old cherries, expert prostitutes, red-heads, lovely, slender Japanese quiffs, voluptuous Persians, hot little Cubans, nurses, ballerinas,
fashion models, amazons, sluts, prudes . . . he could
diddle stenographers on office desks, goose usherettes
during news-reels, play with the sopping pussies of female
diving champions . . . and there was Hollywood, for a
few thousand he could have something really nice . . . He
pictured himself, late at night in the deluxe cabin of some
DC 6, with a naked and stately Greer Garson, making
frantic love as they winged their way high above the
Pacific, to the Olympic Games at Sydney. For a moment
the reality was so piercing that he shuddered – 'Mrs
Miniver,' he could hear himself murmuring, 'Mrs Miniver,
I'm coming!'

By this time he had actually attained the Champs-
Elysées but in such a state of rapture and excitement that
he couldn't make up his mind between the Jaguar, the
plane tickets or a twenty-thousand franc whore, and
simply bought a bag of peanuts and got into the metro.

Twenty minutes later, when he emerged at Place St
Sulpice, the child-choir was still going strong – 'And God
rest you and send you a Happy New Year . . .' they
intoned endlessly, but Trent had calmed down somewhat
nevertheless and his gait was slower and more meditative
as he turned down the rue Ferou and entered the large,
refined apartment house where his 'den' was located. The
'den' was a large room to which only he had the key.
Apart from the cleaning woman no one but he ever
entered it. It was here, surrounded by many Ming
ceramics and T'ang bronzes, and a well-stocked library of
Orientalia, that he spent the major portion of his time.

Automatically, he went into the library and lay down

13

on the black leather couch. He gazed at the rows of Chinese text-books disdainfully. What a farce it was! He'd been coming over here for two years now, seldom arising from the couch, and trying to understand Chinese. He also took courses at L'Ecole de Langues Orientales. In spite of this, there weren't more than a half-dozen Chinese characters that he could even recognize let alone write or pronounce correctly. He wondered why this was. After all, he knew some students at L'Ecole de Langues Orientales who had started studying Chinese after him and who now were capable of holding simple conversations with the professors. Of course, learning how to speak hadn't been his chief aim: he was more interested in being able to read the classics. The only thing wrong with that was that he wasn't able to read too well either; not a bit you might say, because he was still forced to look up every single character in the dictionary and never succeeded in remembering any. Worse than that, it often happened that he wasn't able to find the one he was looking for, so that even at his snail's pace, he still couldn't understand what he was reading, whereas some of those same other students could sometimes read a whole page without once consulting the dictionary. There was probably something wrong with his method which, summed up, was to avoid straining. It had to come smoothly he believed, and all at once. He hadn't minded waiting although it had gotten so he wasn't enjoying the thing very much. If it hadn't been for Vivian, he thought, he probably would have let the whole thing go for a while, but she had been so understanding, had made so few demands on his time, letting him spend long hours in the 'den' every day, and not even protesting when he spent the night there, which he frequently did. She had had such faith in him! Yes, Vivian had been swell. His mother

14

thought so too and told him several times that he was lucky to have married a girl who required so little attention. It almost seemed too bad that he was leaving and wouldn't see her anymore. She was a seductive-looking blonde, too: that probably had something to do with it. He'd always regretted that she was so frigid – it would have been fun if she'd even consented to let her hair down and love it up for a while, but she was always the one to remind him that he needed all his time and energy for his studies.

What was going to be enormously enjoyable, however, was going to be not having to feel guilty anymore – towards her or his mother or the concierge. This latter was cross-eyed and seemed to be silently weeping all the time. Her eyes had a way of taking turns looking at his and welling with tears all the while, which made him feel he was pretty badly at fault about something. What the 'something' was, exactly, was impossible to determine; it was just a moist, hurt, cross-eyed look.

There were quite a few other annoying things too – details of one kind or another – which it would be agreeable to abandon. Vivian's hats for instance. She went in for wearing hats a lot – very small ones – and was quite sensitive about his reaction. He had to be careful always, not to let it be seen that he thought them too small and a bit ridiculous therefore. It would have made her sad and pensive, ruined her day, he supposed, and so he loyally agreed that they were cute, but it wasn't true. There were lots of other things like that – things that were dishonest but that he had to do if he were going to be nice. It was going to be a great relief not to have to be 'nice' anymore.

But all at once he sensed that it would be possible to go right on living with Vivian, as he had been, without being annoyed by all these things anymore. He was free whether he stayed with her or not. The idea intrigued him. To have precisely the same life as before, only this time not to be affected by its disadvantages, seemed even more diverting than May Day in Moscow. He would excuse Vivian. That was all there was to it. She wouldn't know and the concierge wouldn't know but he would have a marvelous secret – he would be doing any damn thing he pleased and not feel the least bit guilty. It was delicious and the children started to sing again: 'No more rulers, no more books, no more teacher's dirty looks.'

As he exulted over this latest discovery, the doorbell rang. He walked slowly to answer it so that his feet resounded mournfully on the marble floor of the ante-room.

Vivian stepped in looking very pale and breathless. He turned without saying anything and returned to the library. He walked in the same funereal way, as if he were numb with sadness, and she followed him penitently.

He lowered himself heavily to the couch and looked at her in a sickly way, his eyes as hurt and extinguished as he could get them.

Unable to confront those terrible eyes, she threw herself to her knees at his feet. She clasped his legs in her arms and pressed her face to his knees, all the time gamely fighting back the tears. 'Oh baby, baby, why did I do it?' she said in a husky voice.

'That's strange, that's what I was going to ask you,' he said.

'WHY did I do it?' she insisted. She sounded as if she really wanted to find out. 'Trent, baby! . . .' She lifted her head as if she were going to say something, then, unable, dropped it to his knees again and began to sob.

There was Vivian crying, he noticed gleefully, and he

didn't feel the least bit guilty. He looked down past the heaving shoulders to the roundness of her derriere, emphasized as it was, by her kneeling.

She looked up again. 'Trent . . .' She was a bit taken aback by the direction of his gaze, but went on as if she hadn't noticed it. 'I must have been insane – out of my mind.' Trent did not move his eyes from her buttocks. He stared at them mournfully and pictured what they would look like naked. 'Trent! Say something to me! Please!'

'I don't feel so good,' he lied.

There was silence for a few minutes, punctuated by several strange little noises from Vivian's throat. Behind his mask of forlornness Trent was feeling real lust. The fact that her eyes were wet with tears excited him, and above all, the fact that she had so hotly and recently committed adultery. Her body must still smell of his maleness.

Trying to catch his eye, she said:

'If only I could explain it to you. I'm such a fool, I should have tried to talk to you before it was too late. Oh Trent, Trent, what are you going to do?'

There was a look of fear in her eyes, he noticed, as if she thought he was going to hit her – almost as if she wanted him to. He had an impulse to burst out laughing, but controlled himself. 'I don't understand,' he said sadly.

'Believe me, I didn't want it to happen,' she said.

'If you *really* didn't want it to happen, I don't see how it did.'

'Oliver isn't nice,' she revealed. 'You think he's your friend, but . . .'

'Thanks,' he cut in drily. 'I figured that out for myself.'

'But you don't know. He's . . . he's a liar.'

'Why? What did he lie about?'

17

'I thought it was just a question of a few kisses. I told him I didn't want to do anything bad and he lied; he told me not to worry because you were his friend and he wouldn't be able to do anything seriously bad because it would be so rotten.'

'I don't see what you were doing kissing each other in the first place.'

'If I told you, you probably wouldn't believe me – it's so stupid, the whole story.' Vivian was no longer crying and the tone of her voice suggested that she thought the danger to be already past and that they would now discuss the matter objectively and dispose of it that way. 'You know,' she said, even managing a little joke, 'it's partially your fault.'

'My fault? How do you figure that?'

'Oh, because of those things you were always trying to get me to do.'

She was referring to the most embarrassing aspect of their relationship: his attempts to make her abandon herself to the act of sex and her refusal to do so.

'I didn't let you know,' she went on, 'but those things you used to suggest, and the things you used to try to do, got me terribly excited. I didn't let you do them because I thought it would be better for you, better for your work, if we didn't; but I wanted to learn how to make love – for your sake – and I was too shy to ask you . . .'

'So you did them with Oliver.'

'Honestly Trent, I swear to you I didn't think it was going to happen. I thought we were just going to kiss and, I admit, I was curious about it – but nothing more.'

'What I'd like to know is how the whole thing got started.'

She lowered her eyes and her fingers fidgeted nervously in her lap as if she were debating with herself whether or not to tell him. 'It's because I'm a woman, I guess,' she said in a small voice, 'and when someone flirts with me . . . well, it's flattering; it does something for my ego.'

'I suppose I know what you mean,' Trent said generously. He was thinking of a book he had just read, by Moravia, about an author and his wife who decide to stop making love because he, the husband, has some writing to do. Everything is going nicely and the book is coming along well when, one night, he hears his wife leave the house and go out into the garden. He follows her and witnesses a sizzling screw between her and the fat village barber. The point is that he loves her so well that he understands that this slimy part of her character is part of her too – her animal part – and he goes on loving her all the more.

'I was alone so much of the time too,' she said, quickly exploiting his consideration. 'Most of the time it was as if I didn't have a husband at all . . . but that's no excuse, I know. God I wish I could take it all back somehow.'

You dirty bitch, he was thinking, you're just sorry because I found you out. 'Listen,' he said, 'I don't think it's anything to get terribly upset about. It happened, and I think I understand why, and now it's all over and I think we should just forget about it.'

'Oh Trent, you're so good. Honestly, I don't deserve you.'

'I don't like to see you crying,' he explained benevolently.

It was working; he was delighted to see: his sense of responsibility was no longer functioning and lying to her was as easy as falling off a log. In spite of the spiritual elevation of his remark, and the saintly set of his features which accompanied it, he found himself once again staring at her body. She still was sitting, curled up at his feet, her

19

head resting gently on his knees and with a peaceful, and rather mysterious smile on her full lips. That quality wasn't confined to her lips – everything about her, her thighs, her hips and posterior, the calves of her legs, and most of all, her round breasts – all of it was like that, swollen a little, more distended than other women's parts. Even the lips of her vagina were plump . . .

He reflected on all this, devouring her the while with his eyes. As always, she seemed in danger of bursting right out of her clothes and, as always, his impulse was to aid her in the process – to undo the one button on her bust which would send the others popping off, to lower the tab of her skirt's zipper a few notches and let her straining waist do the rest. Garments constrained that vibrant body cruelly and he wanted to give it ease. He thought of how she had always refused to allow him such liberties, but, for once, without bitterness. It was very pleasant to have transcended that vexation. He hoped it was gone for good, then he lapsed back into contemplation of the exciting curves of her body. 'Vivian . . .' he began.

'Yes?' she answered dreamily.

'Let's fuck.'

She laughed briefly and somewhat artificially.

'I don't see why you think it's so funny,' he said, pleased with the calmness of his voice. 'You said a little while ago that you were secretly excited by my ideas.'

She laughed again; it was a good joke. 'I can see I shouldn't have been so honest with you.'

It was the same old pattern. Trent paused and checked, a bit apprehensively, to make sure it wasn't making him feel bad. It wasn't. On one level he was behaving exactly as in the past, and on another, and more profound level, he was watching himself behave like that and with complete detachment. Reassured, he returned to the attack. 'Why not? It's good if we can be honest with each other. That's why I asked to fuck – because I honestly felt like it. I think it would be good for us, too, I really do.'

'No, thanks. Little Vivian's had enough for one day.'

'Little Vivian,' he thought. It sounded like a pet-name for her pussy. 'Little Vivian' had had a hard morning with that stiff prong poking around in her, was all pink and sore and couldn't stand to be touched.

She was sitting with her legs curled beneath her, her rump jutting out invitingly. He reached over and placed his hand, with scientific accuracy, low, and in the center, at the exact spot where 'Little Vivian' lay hiding. Her pussy was all sore and he felt sorry for it and wanted to rub it. At the same time, he coolly watched her face. It hardened and something like a shadow flitted across it.

This was being pretty bold for him. Ordinarily, he would have been too worried about her reaction to hazard so blunt a caress.

She said nothing and didn't move.

He began to rub now, gently at first, and slowly, but soon increasing the pressure so as to actually feel, in vague outline, the contours of her sex.

This was too much. She wasn't accustomed to this sort of thing and didn't intend to stand for it. With an abrupt movement, she raised herself to her knees, swinging her bottom safely out of range, then coolly got to her feet. Standing before him, she placed a hand on his shoulder and looked into his eyes. A faint smile played with the corners of her mouth, a smile that was, in part, apologetic, but mostly pitying, and cruelly superior. It was the smile of a saint in a painting, looking at the writhing mass of humanity below, loving them all in equal portion and hoping for their ultimate salvation.

21

This religious attitude failed decisively to have its effect, for he, without a moment's hesitation, grabbed the sides of her skirt by the hem, and, with brutal rapidity, hoisted it to well above her waist.

There, level with his eyes and inches away, was the furry triangle of her pussy. Finding her naked beneath her clothes shocked him: he had forgotten how he himself had witnessed that morning how she had deliberately set out to visit Oliver without bothering to wear panties.

He wanted to press his face against the soft, fair-haired muff of her sex. It was irresistible and he leaned forward quickly, reaching behind with the arms that held the black skirt aloft to better lock her in place. But she was quicker than he. Seeing what he intended to do, she swiftly dropped to a kneeling position again in order to prevent it.

This movement was intended to protect her pussy from his longing; to get it down low and no longer visible, and where her crouching would cover it, shield-like, from his importunate mouth.

It was a big mistake. What she had done, in effect, in putting this distance between his face and her sex parts, had offered them all the more invitingly to his hands. For kneeling as she was, her bare posterior exposed her to a much more insidious attack. He took good advantage of this vulnerability and, in an instant, encircling the lyrelike curves of her hips and thighs with his arms, his fingertips round her genitals and assaulted them – from behind, from underneath, entering into hair and lips and apertures, and moving constantly, like fingers going on a musical instrument of some kind.

'Please! Trent, stop it!' There was a note of panic in her voice as she squirmed away, half falling over, and finally coming to rest sprawled on her side on the floor.

22

A kind of rage struck him and, for a moment, he considered leaping on her from the couch and venting his anger and the years of suppressed passion on her in an extraordinary fit of violence. He thought better of it instantly though. It was much more important for him to preserve his new-won nonchalance than to risk everything for the sake of a few random slaps and cuffs, much as she merited them. Still, strangely enough, he again got the impression, from the look on her face, that this was exactly what she was hoping he would do. Well, all the more reason for not doing it. He distrusted her completely now: the fact that she desired a thing was a sign that it might be dangerous for him and was to be avoided. He was very excited though. The few seconds of liberty that he had had, in which his hands had finally fondled her nether regions unrestrainedly, had been a sharp departure from their usual prudery; and it would have been delicious to go on, if only for a few seconds.

'I couldn't help it,' he said. 'You can't imagine how much I wanted to feel your cunt. I wanted to touch it, to put my finger in it, and I wanted to fuck you and to come. My God, you can't imagine how much I wanted to come! I guess it's from having seen you and Oliver this morning . . . I don't know why, but it's made me terribly lecherous. Oh Vivian, why don't you let me? Right now. Right where you are on the floor. Just lie back and open your legs and let me fuck you. Don't you want to at all?'

Even though he said all this with perfect candour, and even though there was nothing artificial in the pleading quality of his voice, he couldn't help congratulating himself on his hypocrisy. For somehow, he no longer cared what her reaction was, and it no longer mattered very much if he wrecked the delicate balance of their equilibrium. Strangely, this indifference of his made it possible,

23

for the first time, for him to speak to her with perfect honesty about his physical feelings.

She made no attempt to comply with his request but did just the opposite, sitting up with her legs curled tightly together and her hands folded primly in her lap.

'Listen,' she said. 'I've already told you – what happened this morning was an accident. It was very foolish of me and I'd like to try and forget about the whole thing. I'd appreciate it if you'd stop throwing it up to me. I feel bad enough about it as it is without your harping on it. I also think that's a rather strange way you have of reacting to it.'

How could she accuse him of 'throwing it up to her' and of 'harping' on it? He'd only mentioned it once, and it would have been more natural if, like any other husband in the same circumstances, he had not only dwelled at length on the subject of her infidelity, but had also given her a stiff punch in the nose to express his indignation.

It was a typical example of feminine illogicalness and of 'bitchiness.' It was also, he reflected, something he rather liked about her, and women in general, this faculty of being insanely inconsistent. He resisted the temptation to argue the point, therefore, and got back to his original position.

'Okay,' he said, 'I apologize. I guess I was a bit carried away.

3

He lay on the black couch and waited. Slowly, as his eyes
became accustomed to the darkness, the dim forms of
tables and chairs emerged; and, simultaneously, the day's
memories echoed in his mind. He wondered how long he
had been asleep. It was night, obviously, but he hadn't
the slightest notion of how late it might be. Something
important had happened – so important that he felt a
vague terror that he might have forgotten it – but what
was it? He had opened the door and seen Oliver on top
of Vivian, of course, that had been the high spot of the
day and there was no danger of his forgetting that, but
what was the other thing?

He carefully retraced the day's events in an effort to
solve the riddle. He had walked for a long time, he
remembered, after that shocking scene in Oliver's room,
and had finally come to his den. The doorbell had rung
and it had been Vivian. She had told him how sorry she
was and he had excused her and after a while she had
gotten up to leave. She had stood there looking at him
searchingly and he had smiled at her. 'Don't worry,' the
smile had conveyed. 'It's all right. You are forgiven and
you may go home.'

He had lain on the couch and listened to the cruel little
explosions her high-heeled shoes made on the marble
floor as she left; there had been the noise of the door
opening and, as usual with her, it had not shut – she was
incapable of leaving a place without having forgotten
something of crucial importance and having to come right

25

back. This time it had been for cab fare: in her excitement she'd forgotten that she'd left her purse at Oliver's and didn't have any money. He'd given her a five-thousand franc note and there had been the sound of her high-heels on the marble again and this time, after the door had opened, it closed again with a click of finality. He had fallen immediately into a profound sleep. She had been very upset, he recalled, had even cried a bit. The whole thing was so utterly fantastic and the wonder of it was that he himself didn't feel more upset . . . He sat up suddenly with a start of pleasure; the 'important' thing he'd been striving to remember had just come back to him – he was *happy*!

At once he sprang to his feet and made for the door.

Outside, a great autumn fog bleared everything in the city. As he crossed the Place St Sulpice, shoulders hunched against the chill, he couldn't even see the church: the great mass had been totally swallowed up in the thick mist. Here and there a dim glow indicated the presence of a café or of a cautiously proceeding car, but these ghostly lights only accentuated the dimensionless, grey night.

It suited his mood perfectly – this weather – it veiled him from the world and made it possible for him to give full vent to his new identity. Now and again a human form would appear suddenly and pass him by and it occurred to him that, on such a night, it would be relatively simple to quickly grasp a woman in his arms and thrust a hand between her legs, then, almost before she had time to scream, to take three rapid steps and be lost forever in the steaming oblivion. The fog was so thick however that he had no way of determining the sex of the vague shapes he encountered.

He turned left when he came to the Boulevard St

Germain, and passed in front of the Café Deux Magots. It was completely empty but he couldn't be sure whether this was due to the weather or the lateness of the hour. He rounded the corner, and, halfway down the rue St Benoit, heard the sounds of jazz which seemed to be coming from under the pavement at his feet. A closer inspection showed that there was a kind of ventilation grill in the sidewalk and that he was standing on top of one of the numerous cellar nightclubs of the quarter. He groped along another few steps until he found the door. Inside was a red-plush staircase leading down. The music blared up strongly and, mingled with it, he could hear the sounds of clinking glasses and of feminine laughter. He decided to have a look.

The room he entered seemed very small and was jampacked with people. It looked as if everyone in the neighborhood had gathered there to escape from the weird and oppressive fog. On one side of the room were the band and a tiny space where couples were dancing, and on the other was the bar. Scattered about were couches and divans which, for some reason, were mostly empty – everybody seemed to be standing up. He squeezed through a thick knot of people and sat on a couch. A waiter appeared instantaneously, as if he had been waiting a long time for someone to sit down and order a drink, and Trent ordered a *pastis*, lit a cigarette, and began to eye the women.

The room was full of them and they all looked ravishing. It was something he hadn't done in a long time, and it was a real pleasure to calmly and seriously stare at women. For once, there was nothing furtive about it. He took his time, studying their faces, comparing their bodies, observing their movements, with the objectivity and the self-righteousness of a person reading a menu in a restaurant. What was he going to have for dinner?

It was hard to choose. There were so many. And besides, wasn't that the best part – looking at the menu and tasting all the dishes in one's head? Because choosing one meant excluding all the others. He began a little game which consisted of picturing them with parts, or all, of their costumes missing. The tall Spanish-looking one on the dance floor, for instance, whose breasts jumped so electrically each time her partner whirled her away and back to him – it was nothing to visualize her as if she were just wearing her skirt, barebreasted, and without the tight sweater that did so little to conceal the delirious activity that was taking place beneath – or the svelte brunette, standing at the bar with her back to him, who was nonchalantly stroking her hair and who was naked except for her black garter-belt and high-heeled shoes . . . She turned and looked straight at him, as if she had sensed the lustful gaze burning at her rump – and then she smiled.

He smiled back nervously, overcome with embarrassment – it was Margot!

It wasn't just that she had caught the expression on his face as he had stared at her imaginarily revealed derriere – that was bad enough – but that she was Oliver's mistress, someone he was not supposed to have lascivious thoughts about. It was as embarrassing as the time Vivian had caught him standing on the chair peering through the transom at her in the bathtub.

In the next second he remembered joyfully that after what had happened between Vivian and Oliver there wasn't the slightest need for him to feel guilty about anything, least of all about Margot. There was the disturbing possibility that Oliver might be in the place though, since his girl-friend was. He didn't feel a bit like seeing Oliver at the moment. However, a rapid glance at the other people at the bar indicated that Margot was alone, and, as she was still looking at him, he raised his glass and beckoned her to come over and have a drink.

This was a rather unusual thing for him to do, for in spite of the fact that they'd known each other for a long time he'd practically never said a word to her or even looked at her. Oliver and Vivian had always been present and it had always been a question of everyone's listening to Oliver who was a brilliant talker. Trent had been aware, of course, that Margot was exceptionally good-looking (all of Oliver's girl-friends had always been), but for this very reason, and since she *was* Oliver's mistress, and since Vivian had always been there, he had never permitted himself to do anything which might betray a personal interest in her. After all, Oliver was his best friend and it would have been inexcusable to flirt with anyone that was his mistress. Aside from that it would have been downright hopeless considering how successful Oliver always was with women and how little chance he, Trent, would have competing with him. In addition to all this, Margot was a strange sort of a girl, a writer, and very wrapped up in her work, which tended to make her a bit aloof.

Nevertheless, here she was coming across the room, threading her way through the crowd as if there were nothing remarkable at all in his invitation.

For an instant he felt slightly alarmed, wondering how to behave, what to say; but again his timidity vanished as he remembered that he was free to do as he pleased. He looked at her boldly as she finally got to where he was and sat down beside him. She looked like Garbo at the

29

age of seventeen. Yes, he said to himself, you can stop looking at the menu now, this will do quite nicely . . .

'Where's Vivian?'

'Where's Oliver?'

They had spoken together, now smiled at the coincidence.

'Now that we've gotten that over with,' he said, 'what would you like to drink?'

'I'm not sure I should have anything; I've had quite a few already.'

Her knee was touching his lightly. He wondered if she mightn't be a bit tight. He motioned with his hand to the waiter: 'I'll get you a *pastis*.'

'I didn't know you ever came down here,' Margot said, crossing her legs.

'I don't,' he replied. 'Never been here before. I was up there wandering around in the fog and I suddenly got the idea that it might be nice to come down here and get cockeyed.'

'What for? Are you feeling blue?'

'Yes, that's right. I'm feeling blue.'

'I thought so,' Margot observed. 'When I looked over from the bar and saw you sitting here, you had a very strange expression on your face. What's wrong?'

He prudently decided against confessing that his 'very strange expression' had come from picturing her without her clothes on. 'I don't know,' he invented, 'I'm bored, I suppose. I don't have anything to do and it gets pretty boring.'

'What about the Chinese?'

'That bores me too.'

'You know,' Margot said, after a moment's reflection, 'the trouble with you is that you've got too much money.

30

You never need to do anything. Most people are so busy with their jobs that they never have time to get bored.'

Trent thought of Margot's job: the sort of books she wrote were the kind that could be printed in Paris only. 'Is that the way it works for you?' he asked.

She looked him in the eyes for a moment, then answered with sincerity.

'Of course that's the way it works for me. Maybe you think it's easy for a female to write about love – physical love – with brutal frankness . . . going into all the details . . . confessing things that other women spend their lives hiding . . . mentioning things that a girl my age isn't even supposed to know the existence of . . . Maybe you think it's easy, but it's not. As far as I'm concerned, it's the hardest kind of book there is to write – if you take it seriously, that is, the way I do.

'For instance, take an ordinary woman novelist, what does she do when a couple of her main characters go to bed with one another? She describes a couple of kisses, she mentions that the girl's "soft bosom is heaving strongly" and that the man is looking at it and feeling "intense desire," and then he takes her in his arms and that's it – the next thing you know, it's the following morning and they're getting up and the sun is shining and life is beckoning and all that . . . Well, the women who write like that have it easy. They skip the hard part – the true part. They don't say what the characters *really* felt and did. That girl with the "strongly heaving bosom", her pussy was getting wet too; and the man with the "intense desire", he had a big hardon, and what they were going to do about it was going to be a hell of a lot more fun and more important than that little row of dots in the book would lead you to believe.'

Margot stopped to catch her breath and Larry looked

31

at her with admiration. Who would have thought that a pretty little eighteen-year-old had so much going on in her head, and that she'd have the courage to use such coarse words. He looked at the fullness of her thighs, outlined beneath the tight blue skirt, and wondered if she were equally frank in her behaviour.

'I know you're serious,' he said. 'I can tell from hearing you talk. I'd like to read one of your books too, you make it sound very exciting. Are they hard to get?'

'I'll get one for you – but maybe Vivian wouldn't approve?'

'Vivian's not so strait-laced as you think,' he said drily. 'But how about Oliver? What does he think of your writing that sort of thing?'

Margot giggled joyfully. 'Oliver? Are you kidding? He doesn't care about *anything* as long as it doesn't threaten his liberty. He's right too. He's the one who taught me about that – just because people have a lot of taboos and inhibitions about sex is no reason at all why you shouldn't make money at it.'

'Make money at what?'

'At sex. At the fact that everyone's interested in it, wants to hear about it, wants to see it, wants to do it. For me, it works out perfectly: I want to write and I want to write about sex, and that's just what people want to read so I can make a living out of it at the same time.'

'I wish I had something like that in my life,' Trent said with perfect honesty.

'Well, why don't you?' Margot said, sipping her *pastis*.

'Why don't I what?'

'Write a book – the kind I write. It would do you good; it's what I meant before when I said you were bored because you didn't have anything to do.'

'I don't know . . . I've never done any writing.'

'Don't be silly. You can spell, can't you? All you have to do is take a part of your life and write down exactly what happened and, when you come to the sex parts, don't spare the horses – that's what I do.'

'I'm afraid I wouldn't have very much material,' he said wistfully.

Margot looked at him mischievously. 'What's to prevent you from getting some?' she inquired.

It sounded like a challenge. Her face was very close and looking up at him, and her lips looked moist and were parted . . . He wondered if she would duck . . .

She didn't. She did the opposite. As soon as his lips touched hers her mouth opened and pressed against him eagerly. To his amazement, an instant later the soft point of her tongue emerged and boldy sought admittance. A hot flush of excitement rushed through him. He'd been glancing down her low-cut gown ever since she'd been sitting next to him and now, forgetting that they were in a crowded room, his hand raced in and cupped the warm young breast. For a second, he felt her nipple and its hardening tip in the palm of his hand, and then she calmly disengaged herself.

He sat back and said, trying to keep his voice steady: 'For somebody that's only eighteen you certainly . . .'

'Not at all,' she cut him off, laughing gaily. 'I was just showing you how to go about getting "material".'

He wondered whether anyone had noticed them and took a look around. Everything seemed to be going on much as it had before; the dancers were still dancing, the drinkers were still drinking – the room had gotten a bit smokier and that was all. It wasn't unusual, after all, for a couple to kiss in a dimly lit night club. It showed how much he'd gotten into the habit of being a faithful husband, he reflected – he'd kissed Margot and felt her breast a little, and had expected everyone in the room to be staring at them in scandalized astonishment.

'You know,' he observed, 'I think I'd really like to try to write a book like that. Could I count on you to give me a few pointers?'

'I'm always glad to help a fellow artist. Maybe I'd learn something myself for that matter.'

It was too good to be true. He had something going already and he'd only just decided to start looking that afternoon! She was great too . . . he looked at her proudly, as if she already belonged to him. She had that insanely fresh loveliness that girls had when they were just ripening into women. Not long before she'd been a gawky kid probably, thin in the thighs, skinny in the arms and generally angular, and then had come the dramatic metamorphosis, filling out the hollows with that first, young woman's flesh than which there is nothing smoother or firmer . . .

Oliver was very fortunate to have that to play around with. One would think that he would have been satisfied and not found it necessary to extend his activities.

He stole a glance at her. She was watching the dancing couples. He'd have to be careful, he reminded himself, not to let her see how much he wanted her. That could spoil everything. It wasn't going to be easy to hide either . . . that velvet touch of her tongue had brought his joint up like a shot . . . it was agony not to be able to slip it in her right then and there. He leaned forwards, concealing his lap with his forearms, and observed, 'No kidding, I'd really like to try it. And what you said about my needing something to do in life, and needing to make some money myself for once – you don't know how true that is. Besides, after the way you talked about writing, I can see

34

that it must be a damned interesting thing to do. But would you really help me at it?'

'Sure I would. I'll be your tutor if you want. Of course I can just show you the technical part, point out some things to do and some things to avoid doing, but the real stuff has to come from you.'

'That's wonderful!' Trent exclaimed. 'It's really awfully nice of you.'

'Maybe, when you wake up tomorrow morning, you won't feel so enthusiastic.'

'Uh, uh,' he denied, remembering how the satin-smooth, taut skin of her breast had felt in his palm, 'I'm going to feel exactly like I do now.'

They were silent for a while and then Margot sudddenly announced that she was leaving. He said, as casually as possible, that he thought that he too had had enough of the club, and summoned the waiter.

The time had gone quickly and now, as they elbowed their way out through the dense crowd, it took an effort to realize that there had been so many other people in the little room – laughing and talking and existing. He'd been so absorbed in Margot that, for him, all of this elaborate activity hadn't even taken place.

The fog hadn't lifted, he was delighted to note. It lent an air of eery unreality to his walking her home, and, on such a night, things could easily take a carnal turn.

Margot had a room in a little hotel on the rue de Verneuil and they took the long way to get there, going up to the Seine first, and then turning left and walking along the Quai Malaquais.

Trent wondered whether he should try to get her to go down the flight of stone steps and stroll along the river's edge. It was a logical place to go necking with a girl: there were benches to sit on, obscured by dark shadows, and there were the delicate reflections of the street lights, playing on the water, to look at. On a night as foggy as this one, one could do more than simply neck too . . . Still, he didn't like to suggest it. It would be showing his hand. It might be naïve of him to think he could knock her off as easily as that. Better to wait and let things take their course, helping the process in subtle ways. There was plenty of time, after all. No use in rushing clumsily and spoiling everything.

Margot was talking about writing again: it was a subject she never tired of. 'Try and think of a plot,' she was saying. 'It doesn't matter how simple – you can even steal one if you can't think of anything yourself – but you've got to have one to begin with.'

'What's so important about the plot?' Trent said, trying to make his voice sound interested. It was too late to go down the stone stairs now; they had passed the place.

'Because the trick is to get started; and you can't do it unless you've got some kind of story to work with. I say "you can't do it" but of course plenty of writers do – they just write pages and pages about what the characters did and how they felt about it, and how they, the writers, felt about it; and how you, reading the book, are supposed to feel about it. Pretty soon they've got a nice fat manuscript – three or four hundred pages – and the funny thing is that you can read it from beginning to end and absolutely nothing *happens* in it. It's a kind of miracle when you think about it.'

Trent had taken her by the arm as they walked along, but released it now as he stopped to light a cigarette. Instead of continuing to walk when the cigarette was lit, he turned, and resting his elbows on the stone parapet which runs along the river, stood gazing meditatively at the fog-shrouded Seine. 'Why do they do it?' he asked.

'They do it because the safest thing for a writer is not to *say* anything, I mean anything real – how the characters get their motivation, how they . . .'

('Christ!' Trent said to himself, listening to the words pour out of Margot. 'She's talking like a maniac. When is she going to shut up?')

'. . . because if you do that, you're taking a risk; you're saying "this is what I believe," and, after all, people might find that your beliefs aren't very original; they might even decide they're a little stupid . . . No, the safest thing to do is not to say anything, not to let anything happen, avoid having a plot at all, that is. If you throw in enough vocabulary and syntax and all that jive, the reader think's it's *his* fault, and that somehow in that mass of bullshit something is being said which he's too stupid to understand.'

'I don't quite see what you mean though,' Trent said. 'How does having a plot or not having one make any difference if one of those writers you're talking about doesn't want to say anything?'

They were standing facing one another now, and he had absentmindedly slipped a hand inside her unbuttoned raincoat and was casually stroking up and down her side, like a boxer's manager talking to his boy soothingly between the rounds, and all the while massaging his *pectoralis major*.

Margot paid no attention to the hand. It was possible that she was so interested in what she was saying that she actually hadn't noticed it.

'Because,' she replied, 'the plot is what tells you Why. Everything's strung on it like a necklace. All the people in the book get whatever value they have from their relation to it.'

'You're really licked if you don't have a plot, eh?' Trent

contributed. The thumb of his stroking hand extended and rode the bowl of her breast, experimentally brushing the nipple as it passed – Margot didn't seem to mind.

'That's why I say you should even resort to stealing a plot, if that's the only way you can get one, because the rest of it will come by itself later on – I mean the characters and all the detail. You'll probably want to change the plot around for that matter, once you've gotten deep enough into the book, so it really isn't important how you start. You shouldn't have to steal the plot though; it's not hard to think of a story: The Eternal Triangle, Crime and Punishment, The Decline of the Mighty, The Ascent of the Humble, The Comedy of Errors . . . there probably aren't more than a dozen themes in the – , I say old boy, aren't you getting a bit familiar?'

Trent had been listening attentively to Margot's analysis of the novel, but his hand had followed a course of its own and had managed to slip into the shirt where the marvelous young breasts lived. Like a dog in a strange house it had swiftly made the rounds, searching here and there, pausing to tweak a nipple . . . Once again, his knuckles lightly brushed against them. The tender tips grew hard, and it was at this point that Margot had made her remark.

'They're so cute,' he explained, 'I just couldn't resist playing with them a little.'

'Well, you'd better get a grip on yourself. You've got another pair assigned to you in case you've forgotten.'

Her tone was cold and stern: it sounded as if she meant what she was saying and Trent's hand slunk away. He had a moment's dismay, thinking that he might have ruined everything by his premature caress. Would her nipples have protruded so reponsively though, if his fingers had been unwelcome? Wasn't it the same thing as if a female hand had touched him and he had gotten a hardon? Not every female hand would do the trick – it would mean he wanted to make love with the woman who made it happen . . .

'I guess I did forget about Vivian. Do you think that's very bad?' he said, wondering if he oughtn't to tell her about what he had discovered that morning. Did she realize that Oliver was unfaithful? Perhaps it had occurred just that once and she had no suspicion whatsoever on his account. If that were the case and he were to inform her of her lover's transgression, perhaps she would feel disposed to do some transgressing herself; and, since the woman involved was *his* wife, he became an ideal candidate for a partner with whom she could achieve her revenge.

He didn't like the role though. It was informing, and it made it look as if his revelation were simply a tactic whereby he hoped to win what might otherwise be refused. She might quite conceivably have enough spirit to rebel at the idea. Nevertheless, it was a shame that there wasn't some other way that she could find out about Vivian and Oliver . . .

Margot had said nothing in answer to his question and there followed a rather embarrassing few minutes of silence.

'How about pirates?' Trent said suddenly, and a little desperately.

'Pirates?'

'I mean for the plot of my book. How about having a story about pirates?'

'Why? Do you know a lot about pirates?'

'No, not a hell of a lot, but it strikes me it would make

39

a good background – colorful, you know, and plenty of red-blooded action.'

Margot shrugged her shoulders dubiously. 'You're better off writing about something you know. If you don't know much about pirates then you're not going to have anything to say about them.'

'Well, I'd read up on it naturally, till I knew what I was talking about more or less. I wouldn't just plunge into the thing cold like that.'

Trent was actually beginning to consider seriously the idea of writing a novel about pirates. He could gather a small library on the subject he decided . . . it was curious how little he knew about pirates . . . Captain Kidd, that was the only one he could think of at the moment, but he couldn't remember at all what Captain Kidd had done. Was he the one with a hook for a hand? No, obviously that was Captain Hook, or was it Captain Cook?

'. . . you don't get to know anything that way,' Margot was saying. 'It's not a question of "reading up" on anything. I meant that you should write about what you know from your own life.'

'My life is pretty pale stuff compared to Captain Kidd's for instance.'

'What makes you sure?'

'It's obvious.'

'Why? What makes you think that life is different for you than it was for anybody in history, Captain Kidd or anybody else?'

'Well, for one thing, I never raped anybody.'

Margot considered this information a few seconds before replying. From far away there came the sound of church bells, striking the early morning hour. 'If you never raped anybody,' she said finally, 'you wouldn't be very good at describing Captain Kidd doing it. Do you see what I mean?'

'Yes, I see, but it doesn't get me any further. If I'm going to write a book about Captain Kidd I can't re-live his life in order to see what it felt like to be him. All I can do it find out as much about him as I can by looking up his life in books – reading about what he did – there's nothing else I can do.'

'Sure there is.'

'What?'

'Rape somebody.'

Trent looked at her curiously. 'Do you mean you'd really suggest having an experience like that simply to be able to write about it afterwards?'

'What's so shocking about that?' Margot seemed to be in dead earnest. She flipped her cigarette over the wall into the nothingness of the fog and continued: 'Let's face it – the thing that's unique about these particular books is that, for once, the writers have the liberty to deal with sex as frankly as they wish. If they do it well, they accomplish something that's really significant: they throw light on a very, very important subject that's always been a forbidden one for authors. If they don't do it well then their books may be what a lot of people claim them to be – pornography. That's why, if you're writing one, I say you're justified in going to any lengths to acquire the material; and there's no experience, no matter how much it's frowned upon, that you shouldn't pass through if it will help you to understand sex more and make you more capable of expressing yourself about it.'

There it was again – Margot's conception of all things sexual as 'material' for her writings. It certainly was an intriguing idea, he mused, thinking of the innumerable curves of her youthful body. It might also be the solution

41

of how to go about satisfying the hot lust he felt for her. What an idiot he had been not to realize it at once after the way she had kissed him in the club! Instead, he had gone right on trying to make passes in the ordinary way like a high-school kid on his first date. What was called for, obviously, was an objective, 'laboratory' approach. As two writers of erotic fiction, they had a basis for one of the most salacious relationships in modern times – provided, of course, that it was all conducted in the most rigorously scientific manner . . .

'I think I see what you're driving at,' he exclaimed enthusiastically, 'and it's a damn good idea! You mean that if I were writing a passage and I wanted to describe a girl's legs, for instance, and what the man felt like that was looking at them, I'd just lift some girl's dress up, right? and – ' (He stopped and coolly took hold of the bottom of her clothes – raincoat and all – and lifted everything above her waist.) ' – then I could say that, "her thighs were delicious; that the sight of them, showing sleek and white above the tops of her black stockings, made my heart pump faster, that – "' (He placed his hand high on the inside of her leg, just below the lacy edge of her panties.) '" – the skin felt like satin and made me want to feel her legs around me, gripping me like an exquisite trap, pulling me close to her, and forcing me to – '

Margot had thrown back her head in a peal of laughter that was half honest amusement and half nervous excitement. Her teeth were astonishingly white and even; and her lips and open mouth were crimson . . .

'Here,' she said suddenly. 'What have you got to say about that?'

She had stepped back slightly and he thought she was going to let her clothes fall back into place, but instead,

42

she held them up herself and, with a deft movement, she caught hold of the inner edge of her panties and drew it aside, stretching it forcibly, so that all at once her tufted sex was presented to his bulging eyes.

She held herself exposed like that and even strained her lower body forward so as to make her pussy as prominent as possible, and all the while watched, with an unwholesome relish, the eyes of Trent as they in turn stared unbelievingly at this fascinating and yearned-for area of her anatomy.

Then, keeping her dress up with her elbows, she freed one hand and, with a particularly nasty gesture, wet her index finger on her tongue and then lowered it and, very slowly and carefully, placed it at the precise spot on her sex where her vaginal opening was . . .

Trent was having difficulty breathing. He stole a quick glance at her face and caught the evil smile with which she had been watching his eyes.

The finger travelled upwards with infinite care. Around it, the two lips of her moistened cleft parted in an opening furrow like the wake of a ship. When it reached the top of the cleft where the twin lips joined, the finger paused and circled for a while, whirling gently on the little bean of her clitoris. Then it journeyed down again and this time, when it reached the bottom of the groove, it quickly darted into the opening of her sex and half-disappeared before emerging. Then it slipped back in again, and several times entered and came out. She did it in a most obscene manner and with an expression on her face like a bad little girl doing something very dirty and agreeable.

Then, just as abruptly as the whole thing had begun, she straightened up and let go of the elastic edge of her panties. The secret place was veiled again, and she let go of her dress and raincoat so that they both fell back into place.

'You're too much, Margot,' Trent said quietly and with an enormous amount of conviction.

'Why didn't you go on?' she inquired with utmost innocence. 'You were doing very well with your extemporaneous love story. It was very funny too. What made you stop? Did the cat get your tongue?'

'Don't be such a wise guy, will you please? You just caught me off my guard,' he said. It wasn't true though. Just as when she had opened her mouth and put her tongue between his lips, when he had gone to kiss her in the nightclub, she had, this time again, completely capped him by going much further than he had dared to venture, and had succeeded in making him look like a timid imbecile. 'Besides,' he went on, 'I thought we were supposed to be serious about this thing. I was trying out an idea that *you* gave me. I thought you meant what you said.' He sounded hurt, and as if this good faith had been questioned.

'I did mean it,' Margot protested.

But he wasn't listening to her. 'Why are you all such bitches?' he blurted out suddenly in a bitter voice. He hadn't expected to say this and it surprised him a little.

Margot didn't stop to wonder what other 'bitches' he might be referring to. He had spoken spontaneously, and, as with all spontaneous remarks, there had been the ring of veracity in his words. It impressed her, and undid a good bit of the damage caused him by her audacious exhibition and the perturbation with which he'd reacted to it. She looked him squarely in the eye and said gravely:

'Don't think that. I *did* mean what I said. I wasn't making fun of you just now when I did what I did, it was, well, it was the proof of what I was talking about. Don't you see?'

Trent said, 'No. I'm afraid I don't see.'

'All right, it's like this,' Margot explained. 'If you really *were* thinking in terms of writing down what was happening as an incident – the way you said you were – well, I was giving you a "punch climax" for your little story.'

Trent raised his eyebrows dubiously. Her explanation certainly seemed a bit far-fetched and, in any case, he was in no hurry to lose the slight advantage which his pose of outraged innocence was obtaining.

Margot persisted. 'Listen, I *do* think you should try to write. I think it would be very good for you. I was showing you something about that writing-technique I was telling you about – it isn't just your own behavior that gives you the material to write about, it's the unpredictable way that other people react to that behavior. That's even more important for that matter – and besides, did that really make you so angry that I let you see what I looked like between my legs? I thought maybe you might like to see it a little bit.'

Her tone had become insinuating again with this last statement, and a little diabolical. Trent became frightened that she was going to seize the initiative and make him look foolish again, so he allowed himself to be mollified and quickly got back to the subject of his prospective authorship.

'Okay,' he declared with conviction. 'I'm going to try it. I'll start tomorrow as a matter of fact.'

'That's right. The sooner you begin the better.'

'I'm going to need a lot of help though . . . Will I be able to see you about it a few times a week?'

'I told you; I'll be your manager.'

'Great!'

'I tell you what,' Margot said, warming to the role. 'It's a good idea for you to meet Ben right away. He's the publisher. I'll take you over to meet him tomorrow if you want.'

'Yes,' Trent said. 'Tomorrow.'

'That way you can have a little chat with him and get an idea of what it's all about.'

'What's he like?'

'He's not a bad guy – not what you might think. In his way he's a sort of crusader: he's waging a campaign. He thinks that writers should have absolute freedom to deal with the question of love and sex as frankly as they wish, and that the public is entitled to read their books and . . .'

'But what am I going to say to him?' Trent interrupted. She seemed to be beginning another speech and he was getting tired of her verbosity.

'Tell him you're thinking of writing a book. It would be good if you could get a few ideas tonight when you get home or tomorrow morning. Try and write a little outline if you can, or just have something ready in your head that you can talk about. He'll be able to judge whether you can write just from having a conversation with you. He's good at that. If he looks like he's interested you could even ask him for a little advance – that would be excellent for your morale.' She held out her hand. 'I've got to go now. You'd better go home and get some sleep too, otherwise you'll get up too late to do anything tomorrow.'

The touch of her hand shocked him as if it had been some much more intimate part of her body. He suppressed an impulse to pull her to him, to crush her body against his own and roam it passionately with his hands . . .

'Margot, this is awfully decent of you,' he said. He felt in love with her and this polite formula of his gratitude betrayed something much more heartfelt and biological than mere giving of thanks.

'That's all right,' she said. 'It will be good for me too, to have someone to discuss writing with. Give me a ring as soon as you get up.'

Then she left and he started walking home.

4

Trent tiptoed in the blackness of the dark apartment. Expertly he stepped around chairs, avoided tables, placed his hand unerringly on the switch of the hall-lamp outside the bedroom. This gave enough light so that when he opened the door he could see the furniture of the bedroom, the big, double bed, and Vivian sleeping in it.

He approached noiselessly and looked at her. She lay sprawled on her back, legs apart and with her full arms stretched back on the pillow framing her lovely face and the golden torrent of her hair.

Her round, soft breasts rose and fell regularly, and her lips were slightly parted so that she looked almost as if she were smiling in her sleep at some particularly pleasant dream.

'Angelic,' he thought, and her face was so full of peace and innocence that, thinking of how he had spent that evening, for a split-second he felt a twinge of guilt. Then he made a conscious effort and recalled the 'new' state of affairs. Instantly his feeling of guilt evaporated and was replaced by a sense of righteous elation.

He spoke to her – forming the words with his lips and making no sound:

'Do you know where I've been? And what I've been doing? No. You wouldn't be sleeping so nicely. Well, I spent a few hours with Margot. You know? Margot? Oliver's chick. That's right. And you know what? She's got a delicious tongue. You can't imagine how nice it is. I know because I was kissing her a little while ago and she put it in my mouth. It was quite a kiss. And you know something else she has that's very nice? Her cunt. She showed it to me and it's just beautiful. She even played with it a little for me. I bet you wouldn't believe that, but it's true . . . What security you must have, to sleep so sweetly! There isn't a doubt in your mind, is there, that I'm over at the den practising calligraphy with a camel's hair brush; or memorizing the good old 214 radicals; or translating Wu proverbs? – here's a nice one, by the way: "The weak get devoured, the strong are spat out." Isn't that the truth though? Yes, my dear, one has to fight back hard in life, or else one gets walked on . . .

'I've got awfully big eyes for Margot . . . you can imagine – after those things she did tonight. It isn't finished either: I'm going to be seeing her quite a bit now. I'm going to fuck her too. Oh, I'm certainly going to try I'll tell you that. It's not going to be my fault if I don't. You go right on sleeping with your goddamn chastity, and thinking I'm just like I used to be; but I'm cheating from here on in . . . That was your clever idea to go and screw somebody else, and now it's all over is it? Just a silly little accident and we go on exactly as before? Right? No. Not right. Because I'm going to do it too – have a silly little accident. It sounds like it might be fun! And you know, I am getting awfully tired of studying Chinese . . . all those thousands of quaint characters . . . I really do need a little vacation, a little diversion; and thank God I don't have to depend on you this time, you frigid bitch! I'm going to do it with Margot! Do you get that? Going to ball Margot! She doesn't put sex down. It interests her! She likes to talk about it, write about it, think about it and do it! . . .'

* * *

Vivian's dream focused between her luxuriously separated thighs. Ceiling, walls and floor of the room she was in were all fashioned of the same narrow, gray boards – like a seaside bath house, or the inside of a box car, only the room was much larger, was the size of an auditorium.

The man was bearded, and clothed in a mass of animal skins slung carelessly over his shoulders and wound about his neck. He wore the helmet with bulls' horns of the Northern Sagas, and his penis dangled heavily amidst the still bleeding heads and paws of the pelts he wore.

He lifted his hand towards her and made a sign, and she understood that she was to raise her leg high and hold it in the air, bent at the knee, the foot advanced slightly towards him.

He came towards her. There was a great, jagged scar running from his temple to the corner of his bearded mouth. He came closer. His face was impassive. He grasped the offered foot tightly, enclosing its slenderness with his thick fingers. The skin of his arm was smooth and white and piglike.

He turned the foot like a lever, forcing the upheld leg to swing outward, forcing it to the extreme limit of its arc till it strained perpendicular to the axis of her body and she was compelled to clutch his burly shoulders to keep from falling. She was extremely conscious of how her sex organs were being brought into prominence by the strange position she was being constrained to assume. 'If I were naked now . . .' she thought forebodingly, and at that moment, the disaster occurred, and she realized with a thrill of gratitude that she *was* naked. Instantly, his hand lewdly took possession of her unprotected genitals. It was a big hand, and hot, and her sex was squeezed in it like a captured bird.

The man's swinish little eyes danced with mockery now,

and he pressed against her as if to tumble her backwards. She felt the carrion skins he wore rub warm and stickily against her bare breasts.

She had to hop quickly backwards to regain her balance, but he advanced just as quickly, still gripping her foot in one hand and her slit in the other, and made her hop again, and kept on – keeping her moving in this ludicrous manner, circling backwards . . .

There were people watching . . . over the man's massive shoulder, she glimpsed her father shouting at her soundlessly, his mouth contorted with fury.

'I can't help it!' she wailed. 'He's making me!'

The hand holding her foot worked brutally, causing her thigh to swing in until it crushed his other hand still further against her chastised crotch . . . and then out again; in and out; as she clumsily stumbled backwards . . .

Other faces peered incredulously – her younger sister, crying wildly . . . her doctor, making some complicated gesture with his hands – something she was supposed to do to free herself . . . Trent, who was pretending not to notice what was happening to her . . . and strangers, people whose faces she'd seen passing in the street; grotesque faces of old crones and grinning blind men; mutilated faces, faces with goiters; faces with cancers like bunches of huge purple grapes growing from the cheeks; faces with wormy eyes; stump-tongued faces; rotting, decomposed faces of cadavers . . . they drifted round her goggle-eyed, savoring her predicament . . .

The hand that had been clutching her sex released it momentarily and caressed her face with fingers that were not fingers but five slim, tumescent penises that rubbed in her hair and bobbed stiffly against her neck and sought admittance to her lips . . . they crossed and re-crossed her face; she closed her eyes and felt them brushing against her brows and warmly resting on her mouth . . .

There was a sound of waves breaking now, followed by the rushing rings as the water drained away among the shells and pebbles, then gathered again into the next thunderous plunge. She smelled the salt sea and the penises that stroked her face had the taste of brine . . .

It *was* a bath house then. She opened her eyes and saw that one of the gray walls had vanished and the blue sea had been behind it. She lay flat on her back in the sea and her five lovers knelt around her head, hovered over her caressing her face with their erections . . . They were marvelously sweet-tasting and she kissed and licked them fervidly as they rubbed against her lips . . . five young sailors they were, slim lads, whose young rods tasted like dew as she sucked them in turn . . .

But something was gripping her vulva still, and how could that be possible since one hand held her foot tightly and the other with its penis-fingers was fondling her face? She looked then and – it was stupid of her to have forgotten – it was the large, pink pig of course, and he held her pudendum in his firm mouth, and he pushed at her so that she had to hop again to keep from falling . . . It shoved her still more brutally – actually, it was more like a big calf than a pig, and it mouthed her sex with large, gluey lips as if it were trying to nurse – and her nails dug desperately into the coarse pelt on the man's brawny shoulder –

Her face was covered with dark, hirsute testicles and with quivering male prongs, and the big hand rubbed her vulva boldly. All at once, a throb of pleasure, engendered there, thrilled her belly like a warm breath – and then came another . . . and another . . .

He clenched her foot cruelly, forcing her thigh to open

52

wide, and with his other hand he began to slap her full on her burning orifice . . . the throbs came faster and bigger and bigger . . . she could hear the people murmuring excitedly . . .

The throbbing in her vagina became so rapid and intense that it all merged into a single, swelling hotness; then, suddenly, the man stopped pushing her. The hand that had been playing havoc between her legs flew to her side to steady her; and the other hand twisted her foot inwards and pressed it firmly against her sex . . .

'Ooooooh . . .' Vivian moaned in dismay in spite of her sister who was motioning urgently to her, finger on her lips, enjoining her to silence, and, a second later, she urinated copiously on her imprisoned foot.

The crowd became mute; and the hissing of her water was terribly audible until there merged with it the raucous barking of her father, his head flung back in an uncontrollable fit of laughter . . .

Then, looking at herself in the full-length mirror, she saw that she was all alone: her tormentor and the others had vanished; had been spirited off by some exigency which required that the dream simplify.

She lowered her wetted foot and stood, fascinated by the sight of a beautiful drop of urine that clung glistening to one of her pubic hairs. Then she stopped looking at it. She too was disappearing. The mirror was going to be empty. Something was wrong. She stood in the looking-glass now and watched helplessly as her real self dissolved. Whatever it was, was destroying her marvelous dream . . . beastlike, she had become aware that someone was in the bedroom, standing and staring at her. The smile of pleasure that had been on her dreaming face changed to a pout.

'That you?' she mumbled without opening her eyes.

'Shhhhh,' Trent whispered sharply, as if to warn her not to wake herself up.

She was wide awake though, and bitterly angry with him for having torn her from such a delicious world – she was still hot and passionate from what had taken place, and still saw before her the evil little eyes of the man in the bloody furs and felt his powerful hand clenching her sex, pressing her clitoris, crushing and grinding unspeakably against the very heart of her lovely pleasure. It became more and more tenuous in the next few seconds, and, though she strove mightily to retain it, it fled like time itself through her fingers and quite melted away. Vivian was left feeling cheated and very lascivious and that was all.

'Trent?' she said quietly.

'Yeah. Go on back to sleep. I'm sorry I woke you up.'

'What time is it?'

'Pretty late I guess. I'm not sure, three-thirty or four maybe. Go back to sleep.'

'I can't. I'm up now. Besides, I don't feel well.'

'What's the matter?'

'I've been having excruciating cramps all night, and I've got a migraine headache.' This was a lie and Vivian took a particular pleasure in telling it because of her irritation with him. Of itself, her voice didn't betray her ire.

Trent stepped into his pajama pants and said:

'Do you want me to get you some aspirin?'

'Do you know what would be wonderful, darling?' she asked sweetly in spite of her 'headache'.

'What?'

'A cup of weak tea with lemon. I think maybe that would settle my stomach. It's probably something to do with nervous excitement.' That would take him a little

54

while, she thought, maybe long enough. She wanted badly to be alone for a few minutes.

'Right. You don't have a fever, do you?' he inquired solicitously.

'I don't know,' she said.

Trent went to the kitchen and put a small pot of water on the stove. He performed his little chore with utmost goodwill and as part of what he intended to be a general campaign to lull Vivian into believing that he had forgiven her for what she had done that morning and that conditions were back to 'normal'. He didn't want her to suspect that there was something brewing between Margot and him. He was prepared to go to great lengths to keep it a secret. It was going to be an enormous source of satisfaction to him, he knew, to deceive her, and he was going to do it properly; she wasn't going to know a thing about it. He decided right then and there not to tell her about his plans for writing a book since this would have involved revealing his relationship with Margot. He made a mental note as he poured some boiling water in the teapot to scald it to impress on Margot that this business of his writing a book was a very confidential affair . . .

Back in the bedroom, he snapped on a small lamp and handed Vivian her tea. She lay with the sheet pulled all the way up to her brown eyes which stared at him unblinkingly. Her face – what he could see of it – seemed flushed.

'Are you sure you don't have a fever?' he asked.

Vivian sat up and pushed her luxuriant, blonde hair behind her ears. 'Maybe,' she answered. 'It wouldn't surprise me a bit.'

He placed the back of his hand against her cheek and noted that it felt a good deal warmer than seemed normal.

In spite of himself, this contact with her silky skin aroused him. He was already feeling quite lustful after his strange evening with Margot and now, seeing Vivian, warm and disheveled, and picturing how the heat that emanated from her voluptuous body must be warming the whole bed, he longed to strip naked, lift up her flimsy night-gown, get on her beautiful belly and sink into that heat.

He'd had such desires many times in the past and Vivian's response had been consistently negative. Occasionally, she'd let him have his way, but with such an air of grim resignation and silent suffering that invariably, when he, trembling, had managed to penetrate her rigid, unyielding body, he would experience a few seconds of unbearable sweetness and then, almost without having moved, would ejaculate, completely out of control and covered with shame.

Perhaps, if he had been able to hold back and give her the sort of prolonged and versatile treatment that some men were capable of – perhaps it would have changed things. Perhaps her iciness would finally melt as the warm minutes of prodding in her love-pouch accumulated. Perhaps she would become pliant, wrap her arms about him, open her thighs and hump tenderly back at him!

The thought of it was overpowering. Knowing he was doomed to frustration, he nevertheless begged:

'God, it's been so long since we made love . . . honey, don't you want to at all? . . . It would be so great! . . .' His hand slid down from her cheek and timidly brushed the perfectly round globe of her breast.

She tolerated the caress stonily. It was worse than if she'd taken his hand by the wrist and removed it . . .

'Here I am with a splitting headache and cramps and probably a fever. How can you expect me to want to make love? Honestly, is that all you ever think of?' She

56

was looking at his fly. The bulge there left little doubt as to the pitiful state he was in. She considered the protuberance and a slight tremor of disgust shook through her.

'No sense in fooling around,' Trent said. 'If you think you've got a fever you'd better take your temperature.'

'I can't stand taking my temperature.'

'I know, but you've got to be a little less childish. If you're going to be sick, the sooner you catch it the better,' Trent said sensibly. 'Otherwise you'll be spending ten days in bed with the grippe or something, you know that.'

'All right,' Vivian conceded, 'but you've got to put the thermometer in, and then take it out and look at it – it disgusts me.'

There was a curious gleam in her eye as she stated these conditions which Trent was at a loss to understand. Maybe she's enjoying the idea that she's not going to have to do it herself, he speculated. Not that it mattered what her feelings might be . . .

He went at once to get the thermometer before she might change her mind and withdraw this singular privilege.

Searching for it in the medicine chest, the idea of what was about to happen excited him so that he couldn't resist slipping his hand into his pajama pants and fondling his tumid joint a bit. It felt as if it were within inches of shooting off. All that day's erotic events: the sight of Vivian being soundly jazzed; the fantasies of his promenade; what had happened in the den; and then Margot: *her* sharp, young breasts, and the memory of her standing and showing him her slit and, incredibly, *fingering* it brazenly in front of him – all this inflammatory material had converged and was packed into that ready-to-burst erection.

When he came back into the room he found Vivian

lying curled up on her side. Her butt, bulging prominently under the covers, rested on the extreme edge of the bed.

Trent coated the head of the thermometer with vaseline, then knelt by the side of the bed. Vivian had her back turned, and he didn't hesitate to slide his hand into his pajamas again where it clutched hard on his straining organ in preparation for the impending spectacle.

'Ready?' he asked in a clipped, professional-sounding way.

'Be careful,' Vivian admonished in a muffled voice.

He lifted the cover and folded it back over on her so that only her backside was uncovered. Her nightgown had worked up high on her thighs and it was possible to raise it the rest of the way without her having to lift her body.

Vivian kept her legs tightly together so as to cheat him of any sight of her cleft or even the little beard which adorned it. Even so, the sight of her well-fleshed buttocks – so close that he could see the fine golden hairs which peeped out from the central crevice – he all but came off in his pants. He was forced to release his erection though as with one hand he held the thermometer while with thumb and forefinger of the other he carefully opened the cheeks of her bottom and, for the first time since he'd been married to her, was afforded a look at his wife's anus.

He would have liked to have looked at it for a little while – calmly and philosophically. He would have liked to be able to contemplate it, this anus of a very beautiful blonde woman. He would have thought of it being there when she was a young girl of sixteen, how it had always been there so secret and forbidden (had anyone else ever seen it?) that she herself (had she ever even looked at it herself with a mirror?) just about refused to acknowledge its very existence. And yet it was there, proving in a way that was at once charming and terrifying that she was an animal – like a horse, or like a she-wolf . . .

He would have liked to have looked at it but he knew that if there were the slightest delay she would say something, would perhaps become angry and accuse him of being 'degenerate,' and of taking advantage of the fact that she was sick to indulge his unnatural inclinations.

He gave himself two seconds – that was the absolute maximum – in which to look at it freely, after which he would have to insert the thermometer. In those two seconds, in spite of the nonchalance with which he had considered leaving her that morning, in spite of the enthusiasm with which he had begun his campaign to seduce Margot, in spite of the bravado with which he had silently addressed her as she lay asleep, boasting of his infidelity; in those two seconds, looking intently at her anus, he fell more deeply in love with her than ever before. It was beautiful too – like everything else about her. As he inserted the thermometer he realized that he was very close to bursting into tears . . .

He heard the sharp intake of her breath as the tip of the instrument touched her, then something which sounded like a sigh as the small and puckered hole yielded and allowed the foreign object to slide in.

'Not so fast . . . Slowly!' Vivian instructed. And then, 'That's too far, take it out a little . . . No, not that much . . .'

Trent did exactly as he was told, moving the glass tube in and out as ordered. The wave of sentimentality which he had felt a few instants before, and which had been so mighty that it had almost caused him to weep, had abruptly disappeared. Manipulating the thermometer in Vivian's rectum, watching it slide slowly back and forth in obedience to her commands, was such a formidable erotic

59

experience that all feelings other than that of pure lust were driven from him. It looked exactly as if Vivian were being made love to anally by the thin tube. More than that, it was if she herself desired it since it was she who directed its movements.

At this instant, red-faced and with his eyes bulging, Trent *did* look like a degenerate. He knelt in such a way that his stiff member was held between his thighs and, involuntarily, he worked it back and forth in its area of confinement. The thermometer had at last been positioned suitably and he was waiting now for when it would be time to take it out. He knew he was going to come and he was holding back till the moment when, once again spreading her buttocks, he withdrew the glass tube . . .

At the sight of her anus contracting as the thermometer came clear it finally happened to him. It was a powerful jolt, hitting him violently like an electric shock and forcing him to double over.

He fancied he saw a spasm shake Vivian's body also and make her arch her back, but it was no doubt a trick his eyes were playing on him, blurred over as they were with his ecstasy.

He feared she might suspect something on hearing the sudden movement he had made as he doubled over, so, with the orgasm still pulsing in him, he managed to twist the thermometer and focus his eyes until the thin column of mercury caught the light.

'Well, thank God for that,' he gasped, 'it's normal.'

5

He awoke with a start the next morning. It was 11! He'd set the alarm for 9.30. Hadn't he heard it? Or hadn't it gone off? And where was Vivian? He sprang out of bed furious and full of anxiety. Margot had said she'd take him to meet Ben in the morning. He had to call her at once – perhaps there was still time.

Vivian was in the salon listening to Haydn's 'Clock Symphony'. An empty cup posed on the radio showed that she'd already had her *café au lait*. 'Morning, darling,' he mumbled, dashing for his toothbrush (she was home then – he'd have to phone Margot from outside).

He dashed cold water on his face and remembered with despair that he was also supposed to think of a title and plot for his book before meeting Ben. With a mouthful of water and toothpaste foam he tried to give the problem some thought. Nothing happened. No plot and no title occurred to him. He had a slight hangover too which wasn't helping matters. Coming out of the bathroom he walked with exaggerated casualness, then, out of sight, dressed with feverish haste, and a few minutes later yelled from the kitchen:

'Christ! Isn't there any more coffee?'

'I was just going to make some for you,' Vivian lied. 'It will be ready in two minutes.'

'Forget it. I'll go down and get some in the café,' he volunteered craftily. 'I'm dying, I've got to have a cup immediately.'

It looked as though Margot had overslept too from the time it took her to answer the phone and from the tone of her voice when she did so.

'It's half-past eleven. Can I come by and get you right away?' Trent said.

She agreed sleepily and he left the café and hailed a cab. On the way over, he made a fresh attempt to get some idea for a book. This time his brain managed to grumble and squeak and come up with a suggestion. It was vague, but rather interesting. He decided not to push his luck and try to get it any clearer – better to let it ripen by itself for an hour. There was the title though . . . Here again his effort wasn't fruitless and he jotted it down in his address book – 'The Rubber Boyfriend' – it was essentially in conformity with the idea he had which was to write an extravagant satire lampooning the sexual mores of big-city life, full of bizarre objects and colorful details.

When he got to Margot's hotel room he tapped discreetly on the door. There was no answer and he let himself in. She had fallen asleep again after speaking to him on the phone. He drew back the drape from the single window, flooding the room with the strong morning light.

'Right,' Margot said, rubbing her eyes and then stretching her arms high over her head.

He drank in the sight of her armpits, so unbelievably soft, and ornamented with silky locks of hair. There was much more to see in a moment for when she got out of bed her nightgown was so transparent that she might as well have been naked. He sat on the edge of the bed and tried to appear casual at the sight of all those revealed firm mounds, the rose-tipped breasts and firm posteriors and the magnetic black patch nestling between her thighs, but his heart thumped wildly.

It was all he could do not to arise and push her roughly on the bed and sink his hands and mouth into those various and delectable portions of her body, but he had learned his lesson the night before – he knew that he risked losing everything by such a frontal assault – and so he sat still and even pretended to avert his gaze as she hurriedly dressed, irrevocably clothing and concealing her charms one after the other.

Ben's office was within walking distance and, on the way, Margot briefed him as to what his attitude should be with the publisher.

'He's not at all what you might think,' she explained, 'not commercial, not interested in getting rich and the hell with everything else. He has two interests; one is helping new writers to develop, and the other is to fight the taboo on treating sex truthfully in books. After all, there is something odd in the fact that writers are forbidden to deal with what's probably the most important single subject in existence. People like Kinsey and Havelock Ellis make an attempt to report on people's sex-habits, of course, but there's a big difference between that kind of dry, statistical, case-history approach, and the sort of living description that a novelist can get. Don't you think so?'

Trent was fully in accord.

They arrived at this point. She steered him into a building and they walked up a flight of stairs and entered a door. The office seemed modern and efficient. Two remarkably pretty girls sat behind desks and clattered sporadically on typewriters.

'Jacky and Lila, this is Trent,' Margot said by way of introduction. Jacky was petite with big eyes and sharp, pointed little breasts that seemed about to puncture her tight green sweater. Lila was a sullen-mouthed redhead with a creamy complexion. She was taller than Jacky and appeared to be English. Trent wondered if they sized him up to be a writer and it made him feel a bit uneasy. If they hadn't both been so pretty he wouldn't have been so nervous, but they were, and he found himself speculating about them. Were they just ordinary secretaries or were they at all involved in the rather special type of business which their boss was engaged in?

He didn't have time to pursue this interesting chain of thought any further as Margot had already crossed the room and was opening another door and beckoning him to follow her.

Ben seemed surprisingly young to be a publisher. He was good-looking and dynamic and, as Margot entered his office, was seated on the corner of a desk piled high with manuscripts, letters, catalogs and papers of all sorts and was engaged in conversation with a swarthy gentleman who had fine gray eyes and a magnificent waxed moustache. Trent judged him to be forty, but he could have been much younger or much older since it was one of those ageless faces conferred on their owners by great wisdom or remarkable health or both.

'Hallo, Ben,' Margot said. 'This is Trent, a friend of mine.'

Ben got off the desk and came over to shake hands and, as he did so, felt a disagreeable and prickly sensation in the palm of his hand. At the same time there was a loud and vulgar sort of noise.

'Well, for Christ's sake – ' Margot began, and the swarthy gentleman sat forward with a startled expression, but Ben took the practical joke like a good sport and the matter went no further.

The dark man got up and offered Margot his chair, and, evidently having concluded his own business and not wishing to intrude on the new visitors, paused as if wondering to shake hands or not; decided not to, said goodby with a Spanish accent and left.

'Faustino Perez,' Ben said, indicating the departed guest.

'Oh, so that's him,' Margot exclaimed. 'He's the author of *Until She Screams*,' she explained quickly to Trent. 'It's the best book in the series – a parable with a Mexican setting – it's brutally frank.'

'Yes, he's a very strange man,' Ben said musingly. 'He dropped in out of the blue one day with the manuscript of *Until She Screams* and then completely disappeared without even bothering to find out if I were going to print it or not. This is the first time I've seen him since. He's thinking of writing a new book and wanted to know if I were interested. Naturally I told him to go ahead.'

Margot licked her lips and said, 'That book of his gave me gooseflesh when I read it – I wish he hadn't left so quickly. I'd like to have gotten to know him better.'

'You two would make a lovely couple,' Ben observed dryly. 'He's old enough to be your father.'

'Maybe you have to be that age before you find out some of the things he knows,' Margot answered. She seemed to be seriously considering the idea of getting to know Faustino Perez better and Trent felt a sharp pang of jealousy. Margot broke off her reverie after a few seconds however, and told Ben the reason for their visit.

'I see,' Ben said when he heard that Margot's friend was a budding young author. His shrewd eyes appraised Trent for a moment before he inquired, 'Can you tell me a bit about this book you're thinking of writing?'

'What I have in mind is a satire on the Kinsey Report,' Trent replied briskly. 'The hero of the book is a sociology professor – a man about 40, very straitlaced, a bookworm. Kinsey assigns him to do research on the sex-life of the people that live in Greenwich Village – the bohemians. It's undercover work; he's not supposed to let on what he's really up to. Kinsey tells him to pretend to be an artist so that he won't arouse suspicion and to get to know as many people as possible and on an intimate enough basis so that he can discuss their private lives with them, or even observe them in action. Kinsey wants to know what's really going on in the sex-life of the *avant garde* and this professor is his spy. What are the latest fads in sex? What are the newest discoveries? What are the extreme limits of strange sexual behavior? He's supposed to get all these answers. He gets an unlimited expense account. That's his operational method – anyone that's free with money can make a lot of friends in Greenwich Village. Kinsey also supplies him with a lot of secret new drugs and chemicals – aphrodisiacs, truth serums, things to break down people's inhibitions. So that's it – you have this professor with the character of an old maid from Philadelphia geting involved with all kinds of weird homosexual midgets and Japanese nymphomaniacs and Puerto Rican lesbians and everything you can think of, and of course he's profoundly shocked and upset but he has to keep pretending that he's a freak himself in order not to alarm the subjects of the investigation.' Trent stopped and sat back in his chair. He was quite proud of himself. He'd spoken well in spite of the fact that he'd been making the thing up as he went along. He wondered why it had been so easy – probably because the whole idea of writing a book was unreal and quite ridiculous; if it had

66

been something that really mattered to him he would have stammered and been tongue-tied.

'Yes,' Ben said. 'That's not a bad idea. It could be quite funny if it were well done. I haven't published any humorous books as yet but I think I'll go along with this one. After all, humor is a valid medium for getting the truth across. Here's a little advance. Get to work right away and let me see the first twenty pages as soon as they are finished.'

With this encouragement, Trent was able to face up to the pretty secretaries in the outer office more confidently. He gave them both a cold, appraising stare as they walked out as if the whole question of their future relations depended on whether he, Trent, considered them attractive enough to make a pass at.

'What are you going to do now?' Trent asked Margot when they were in the street. 'Do you want to get a drink someplace and talk about our books?'

'I don't think I have time,' she replied. 'Oliver's expecting me over at his room for lunch.'

Trent tried to conceal his disappointment. He'd hoped to spend the afternoon with her. After what had happened the night before he was very hot for her and was dying to get her off alone someplace and continue with their literary experiments. There she was, walking beside him, young and luscious with her taut breasts jiggling rapidly under their sweater and her small waist, proud-sweeping hips and thighs and round buttocks, all within reach of his craving hands – and she was going to leave! It was too sad. I'll get into you, you little bitch, he promised himself, if it's the last thing I do.

They rounded a corner and turned on to the Boulevard St Germain. Just ahead of them was a café – The Old

Navy – and, seated alone on the terrace, was Faustino Perez.

Instantly Margot clutched his arm and said, 'Well, maybe there's enough time for just one drink . . . Oh, look who's here.'

She practically shoved Trent up to the table and then stood devouring the seated man with her eyes and left to Trent the task of making the verbal gambit.

'Hallo there . . .' he said obediently and a bit lamely. Perez regarded them blankly for a few seconds as if he'd already forgotten them, then sprung to his feet with youthful agility.

'Ah yes,' he declared, 'you're the nice young couple I just met at the publishers.' He shook Trent's outstretched hand, then turned to Margot. His look at her was brief but very thorough, taking her in from the tips of her toes, up her legs and torso, stripping off immediately all superfluous garments and underclothes. Margot felt a hot little sting in each of her nipples as his eyes came to, and passed her breasts, as if she really were naked, and as if the beam of his regard were a tangible thing like sharp antennae lightly mounting her and making her want to scratch herself. He looked her in the eyes an instant and his nostrils dilated slightly as if he were inhaling her – then it was over. It had taken exactly one second and had made her break into a light sweat. She slumped limply into the chair he held for her and sat looking as if she'd just received a sizzling slap in the face.

None of this was lost on Trent of course, and he sat down wearily as if *he* was the one that was in his forties instead of Perez.

The man didn't seem to notice that neither of the young people were capable of speaking for the moment, and, ordering a round of white wine, launched off into an amiable chat with Trent about writing, life in Paris, the political situation and various other topics to all of which Trent replied by occasional nods and grunts, sipping his wine nervously and trying not to look at Margot too often. She, seeing she was being ignored, perked up and slung her arm behind her chair with an angry little glint in her eye. This gesture had the effect of straining her right breast in the direction of Perez, inches away, and it was so firm and tight as it boldly stretched against her sweater that it seemed like some kind of weapon she was aiming at him. He acknowledged the threatening globe, glancing at it and pursing his lips, but very courageously not losing his composure as if even if it really did explode and send its nipple through him like a bullet, which seemed possible, that he was not afraid to die. After a moment, he looked her in the eyes again, rather blankly as if he were considering something. Under his gaze, Margot's aggressiveness quickly ebbed away and her eyes became warm and beseeching and said 'yes' a great number of times to whatever it was that he was turning in his mind.

Trent was particularly hurt that she didn't seem to give a damn that he was sitting right there and seeing it all. It was painfully obvious to anyone who happened to be watching that Señor Perez had only to rise and, with the merest flicker of his eyes for a signal, to have her get up and follow him to wherever he chose to go, there to engage in unspeakable obscenities. When he did get up shortly after, however, this flicker was not forthcoming and Margot remained obediently in her seat.

They both looked after him as he walked away – Margot longingly and Trent with envy. His carriage was smooth and graceful – there was no doubt about it, he had a superb body, the muscles small but proportioned perfectly.

When he had disappeared, Trent looked at Margot with an expression that was part humble, part mutely inquiring.

'Yes,' she said with candor in response to his unspoken question, 'I certainly would love to go to bed with him . . . he's fantastic, can't you feel it?'

He had to admit that he could, although it was just seeing her behave like that that made it seem so evident.

'It isn't just the way he is,' she went on, 'it's that damn book he wrote. No woman could read *Until She Screams* without feeling like a bitch in heat. I'm not the only one you know. Don't you know those girls in the office feel the same way? I bet they wet their pants when he walked in.'

She sat back with a sigh and then, suddenly, with the optimism of her eighteen years, shrugged off the oppressive mood that Faustino Perez's presence had engendered in her. There was also, lurking behind this quick change of spirits, that queer and feminine assurance that this man she so desired was now aware of her existence – and willingness; and that he would avail himself of the opportunity in due time.

She now completely dropped this topic and began to talk to Trent about her book with great animation. It was, she revealed, a novel about incest. She'd chosen this subject because, due to the unparalleled pressure against it, stemming from the most powerful of taboos, incestuous love contained a reciprocal force placing it far above all other erotic relationships in intensity. The situation in her book involved a brother and sister – she eighteen and he in his mid-twenties (the same ages as she and he, Trent immediately noted). Their affair had begun in childhood and in utmost innocence – the usual bathtub curiosity, nocturnal investigations, and so forth. Bit by bit, they

70

grasp that this sort of thing is 'naughty' and not to be engaged in except with the utmost discretion. At one point, when he, the brother, is fifteen and the sister is nine, a climactic scene has occurred – the parents arriving home unexpectedly in the middle of the afternoon discover them in bed together naked. Despite their lame excuse of 'taking a nap together' they are severely punished, something which is particularly humiliating for the boy because of his greater age. After this experience, they cease their clandestine kissing and caressing; but it is from fear alone and they continue to be enormously aware of each other physically – even more than before because their desires are suppressed. They grow up like this, each one turning to the other and finding there the logical target of their awakening libidos. The situation becomes more and more intolerable – the sister has become a very beautiful girl, much more beautiful than any other he knows; and he is handsome and in the full fluoresence of young manhood. Added to this, each knows the feelings of the other since rarely a day goes past that they don't exchange a secret all-meaning glance like prisoners in a jail.

She starts the book at this point and the plot quickly develops to the day where the brother finally crosses the Rubicon and lays a hand on her. The main part of the book describes their life and feelings afterwards. They haven't actually engaged in coitus, but every passing day finds them getting bolder. They are both very afraid of course, being both of them at an age to understand the gravity of what they are flirting with, and, since their parents are constantly in the house, there are few occasions on which they dare to succumb to their great temptation. But there are brief and passionate encounters in the hallways when they find themselves suddenly in

71

each other's arms, kissing hungrily with open mouths and then his hands stray instantly beneath her skirt, fondling and frantically searching out the hot forbidden lips between her legs – then, in an instant, as if overpowered by the heat of their craving, they abruptly break off and walk in opposite directions, hearts thumping wildly and with fear.

Margot had gotten quite worked up talking about her book. Obviously, she was fascinated by the idea of incest and even admitted, wistfully, that had she had a brother she would certainly have taken the appropriate measure to satisfy this interest. As for the book, she thought she had a chance to write a decent one but was bothered by the fact that she wasn't able to apply her famous theory, to actually have herself the experiences of her characters, that is, in order to describe them in the most faithful manner. 'That's where you come in,' she said suddenly.

Needless to say, this remark made Trent feel very well, and the glow of excitement increased in him as she went on to explain that her affair with Oliver was of no use to her in this matter since Oliver had the legal status of her lover and what she was after was the way one felt when engaged in an extremely illicit liaison.

This was so much what he'd been hoping to hear that he frowned a little, pretending to be having difficulty following her ideas. As a matter of fact, far back in the conversation, when she had first mentioned the fleeting and secret caresses of her hero and heroine, he had reached under the tiny table (both of them were leaning forward over it), and managed to get his hands between the knees of her legs which were parted a bit since her feet were both rearwards and resting on their toes, the heels free of the shoes, as girls with high heels often do when seated. His hands were joined as if in prayer, or like a diver's, and he'd been wedging them ahead cautiously all the time she'd been talking. When she said, 'That's where you come in,' he lunged forward a whole three inches, almost striking his chin on the table, and felt the satin flesh of her thighs above her stocking-tops.

'That's too easy,' she said moving back in her seat so that her legs slid past him till his hands were once again between her knees, and went on to explain that what she was interested in was the feeling of erotic pleasure combined with, and heightened by, the fear of imminent discovery by some authority such as a parent, or, as it turned out in this case, Oliver, who would thus fill the role of her parents. In other words, Trent could do whatever he liked to her providing Oliver was there or in the very near vicinity.

'How will we do it?' he asked, as if he were trying to look at the thing like a practical problem.

'I don't know, it's up to you mostly. Lots of times we're all together and it will be just like a little game we're playing,' Margot said vaguely.

'All right,' Trent consented. 'I think I see what you mean, but promise me one thing.'

'What?'

'If you know it's going to happen, I mean if we've got a date to all have dinner together or go to the movies or something like that, then I think it would be a good idea if you didn't wear any underwear.'

Margot looked a bit condescending and said, 'Naturally. You didn't have to ask me that, it's what I had in mind. The girl in my book *never* wears underwear.'

With this important point settled, there didn't seem much left to talk about. As on the previous night, Trent deemed it advisable to control himself as much as possible

73

and therefore made no further attempt to touch her or to persuade her to spend the afternoon with him rather than Oliver, and, after a few minutes of silence, Margot got up and said she had to leave. Trent stood up and shook hands without saying anything, and it was she who was forced to inquire about the future.

'When will I be seeing you?' It sounded somewhat chilly, as if she didn't care too much whether she did see him or not.

'Well, when are you going to be with Oliver? I'll try and catch you together next time.'

'I'm usually there in the afternoon and in the early part of the evening. When we go out we almost always go to the Tournon.'

'Right. I'll come over within the next few days sometime,' Trent said casually.

Then she was gone and he was sitting alone at the table sadly watching her adorable backside as it got smaller and smaller on the Boulevard and finally disappeared altogether down the steps of the Odéon Métro station.

He sat back and gave himself over to reflecting about the situation. In the light of what had happened on the previous morning it might seem a little strange for him to drop in on Oliver so nonchalantly. Not only strange, but downright disagreeable. But, and it was a very big and adequate 'but,' in the light of what was happening between him and Oliver's mistress, such a visit was very called for, and promised to be not disagreeable at all but extremely amusing. He'd just have to act like a man of the world, accept graciously whatever excuses Oliver might proffer, snap his fingers at the whole incident as it were, and that would be the end of it. Only it wouldn't – not by a long shot, because he had a lot of plans in mind for 'the little game' Margot had proposed, and already he was toying with an entirely new idea: if he were going to help her gather experiences for her book, it seemed only fair that she should return the favor and *that* could lead to some very interesting possibilities indeed.

6

Trent sighed and rolled over on the couch. He hadn't expected to sigh and it startled him a little. The sigh (not that he bothered to analyse it) was one of physical protest rather than longing or sadness – his body was tired of lying on the couch. Since he'd spent the greater part of four days – ever since Margot had left him sitting at the little café – turning and tossing on this couch, it wasn't surprising that that it was beginning to become a bit uncomfortable.

He was 'working on his book.' He'd decided to get to work immediately as Ben had suggested, and while his ideas were still fresh. Never having written a book before he wasn't quite sure how to go about it. Obviously the thing to do was to retire to his 'den' and figure everything out. This presented no problem since it was what he was in the habit of doing anyway, to study Chinese, and there was therefore no reason why Vivian needed to be informed of the project. He preferred to keep it from her since he had decided that his whole existence was going to become something quite different from what she thought it was – especially his relations with Margot and anything else in that category which might happen to arise.

With such thoughts in mind he had arrived briskly at his private flat firmly resolved to set to work. There was only one trouble – he didn't know what to write. He had, of course, formulated a number of general ideas having to do with the task, had determined, for example, that the way to go about it was to set himself a certain number of pages as a daily stint so that the book would progress steadily. He had thought at first of ten pages as a likely number, but at the end of the first day's work, having done none, he reduced this to five.

The difficulty, as he soon understood, is that you simply can't sit down and tear into a book which you've done practically no thinking about. What he'd told Ben had been all well and good but wasn't enough to fill three pages, and he couldn't think of anything else. Besides that, it had simply been his elucidation of his *idea* and, as such, had no place in the book itself.

No, what was required was to 'think the thing out,' to invent a plot and characters and to make an outline from which to work. As soon as he had thought of the word 'outline' he had gotten up from the table which had become rather irritating with its pencils and typewriter and blank paper, and characteristically, had shifted his center of operations to the couch.

Stretched out comfortably on the familiar black leather, he concluded that, just as with studying Chinese, there was no sense in being in too much of a hurry. Writing was a serious affair, many people spent their entire lives working at it – there would be no harm in spending a bit of time in simply reflecting about it abstractly. It might even be good to concentrate on not thinking about it at all – to think of anything else he cared to and in this way encourage ideas to mount from his subconscious mind and suddenly insert themselves into his day-dreams the way one tries to remember something by 'thinking of something else.'

A further reason to justify lying on the couch and *not* thinking about what he was supposed to be doing was that if he were going to write a book it was important to get his own ideas in order. After all, it was his mind that was going to create this book and his mind, he had to admit, was in a rather confused state. Before beginning the book it would help immeasurably if he could decide just what he thought about life, the world, the people he knew, himself and a few other things. Himself – that was the crucial thing . . . he had to get to know himself first of all.

He tried to look at himself as if he were someone he knew casually. Not a very original person he observed, no pronounced likes or dislikes, not very happy with his wife – but who was? Had never done anything dangerous or important, had no convictions, didn't want to do anything particularly in life, didn't have to, didn't have many friends, didn't like people very much, didn't have much patience – it was quite a negative portrait. 'All right,' he had reasoned skillfully, 'then the book has to be negative.' But what did that mean? What was a negative book?

Whatever it was, it didn't seem to have very much to do with the book he had described to Ben, the Kinsey satire. Better forget all those philosophical inquiries then, and get back to the original idea. It wasn't a bad idea he reflected, trying to generate a little confidence, Ben had said it had humorous possibilities. What about making up a list of fantastic characters – the 'freaks' that his hero was going to encounter? Once he was provided with a likely group he could then proceed to improvising the incidents and intrigues that would relate them, just a if they were a collection of puppets and he the master manipulating them. This appealed to him: it made a game of it and dispersed the grim feeling which had begun to attach to the idea of writing the book and make it seem a more and more formidable task.

He arose briefly – just long enough to get a pad of paper and a pencil – and swiftly returned to the black-leather sanctuary where, after a certain effort of imagination combined with a remembering of some of the odd types he had run into in his life, he compiled a tentative list of people.

First of all came the hero, the sociology professor. Trent decided to call him Mr Edgar Paulson which sounded appropriately academic and serious he thought. He was to be the only normal person in the story and would afford a contrast with the colorful group that were to populate the book.

Next was a massive Negress addicted to holding up candy stores and filling stations. She answered to the underworld nickname of 'Sardine'. Two hundred pounds of amorous, mischievous wickedness, she was accustomed to getting her way and, to this end, always carried with her a briefcase containing a dismantled machine gun. She readily uses this weapon to force reluctant lovers to succumb to her desires. The professor is one of her victims. 'Say "I love you,"' she shouts at the terrified scholar, furiously assembling her machine gun, after he has invited her to his flat with the idea of questioning her about her private life.

Then, Jesse the voyeur. Jesse is a middle-aged New Yorker. He works at the Coney Island amusement park in the Fun House. Inside there is an amazing hodge-podge of tilted rooms, mirrored labyrinths, sliding bridges, trap doors, and the like, and spotted about the place are secret air-jets in the floor for blowing the girls' skirts up. Jesse pushes the buttons that work the jets. From his private booth he surveys the place, sees the girls that have just entered, watches their progress up the stairs of the steep and well-varnished slide. Down comes a blonde high-school girl, sitting on her mat and screaming. Jesse is impassive and hardly seems to notice her, but just at the moment when she pops off the bottom of the slide and stands trying to catch her balance, Jesse's thumb moves viciously and, with a whoosh, her navy-blue, pleated skirt is flying up over her face and she is crouching desperately and trying to hide the fact that her panties are transparent. Jesse is very happy.

'Ricky', the Puerto Rico lesbian. She is the manliest person in the neighborhood. If a chick gives Ricky a fast answer, she may find herself trying to get up from the floor a moment later. Ricky is wanted by the police for killing a sailor with a chair during a fight in a bar. She's about 5 ft 2 and wears her hair slicked back like George Raft.

Jimmy O'Neil, the fag and kleptomaniac. He has a way of shyly smiling at the salesgirl while he is skillfully boosting a pair of pigskin gloves from her counter. He is constantly shopping. When it's suppertime he goes to the supermarket and when he comes back, not one of his thirteen pockets is empty.

Dick, the exhibitionist. One of his low tricks is to stand directly in front of young girls on the subway; then, at a given moment, he allows his overcoat to open just enough to reveal his joint, rigid and sticking out of his fly. They are always terribly embarrassed since he is gazing casually in some other direction and seems as if he really mightn't know that his pants are open and member exposed. At any rate they never do anything but just sit there and blush, and even steal a glance out of sheer curiosity at the famous penis. 'So that's what it looks like,' they think, and proudly describe it to their twelve-year-old friends amidst gales of giggling.

Sadistic Pierre. Everything he does is calculated to hurt somebody. He deliberately steps on people's feet when he is sidestepping through an aisle in a movie. He spends hours gazing out his window hoping to see an automobile accident. Frequently, he loiters about funeral parlors because he loves to see people crying. He's very fond of animals and is constantly picking up stray cats and dogs and taking them home with him, but none of his pets last very long.

'The Bastards Athletic Club', a local gang of tough teenagers. They roam about the Village in groups of six or seven, several of them wearing their official windbreakers – orange with black sleeves, and with 'Bastards' sewn on the back in blue. They like to catch women late at night and rape them in deserted parking-lots. Many of them are trying to ignore the fact that they are faggots.

A couple named Florence and Bert who like to make love in public. In the street he bends her over backwards and the passers-by can see their jaws and tongues laboring in an old-fashioned french kiss. Then they straighten up and stride joyously along, he with his hand encircling her bub, she with her hand in his side pocket. If they are at a party, they get much bolder. It is so common to see Florence mounted on Bert as he sits in a chair, or Bert sprawling on Florence on a couch that nobody even stops to verify if they are actually having intercourse or not: if they aren't it is because they've just finished, or haven't begun yet. When they are at home and alone together they spend all their time reading.

Trent decided he'd better add a couple of pretty girls to the cast for the sake of any reader who might find all this a bit boring. Immediately, Vivian and Margot suggested themselves as models. A blonde and a brunette – it was so inevitable! But what sort of sexual manners should he attribute to them? He realized that he'd only the vaguest idea of what the two women in his life *really* felt about love-making. He couldn't imagine what it felt like to be frigid like Vivian – to be bored with sex as if it were some complicated sport in a foreign land where the player wears a costume that is somehow shocking and tedious. Nor did he understand Margot's rule of having to pretend that she and her lover were characters in a novel's torrid plot. It didn't matter though; since the way they *appeared* to be would do quite well for his book.

After a while, he thought of a name for Vivian. It was 'Catherine Cornball' which expressed his spiteful resentment of her Presbyterian inaccessibility. But when he tried to think of words to describe her body he became less flippant and an awkward feeling of dread lurked in his chest. It depressed him. It was a sign that she still affected him mightily. He began to think of how she had perfumed between her legs on the morning of her assignation, and the thought was so painful that he nervously interrupted it and focused his mind on Margot.

Margot was so young, and her habit of abruptly doing things that were shockingly carnal was so intriguing, that, thinking about her, he easily forgot his morbidity of a few seconds before. It had been days and days since he'd seen Margot with her slim waist and bold breasts. It had cost him an effort but he was playing the waiting game. He had given himself an order when last he'd seen her – 'Let there be days now, before she has me coming to her again whimpering with a hardon!'

But now, there *had* been days: he'd served his penance and it was going to be time to see if his self-discipline was to be rewarded.

He got up excitedly and ran his fingers through his hair and put the pad, with the list of characters, on the table. He did it with unconscious finality. He was on his way out of the house but hadn't realized it yet. When he did, he had a twinge of remorse. He'd spent four days now working on the book, and he should have had forty manuscript pages to show for it according to his original scheme. Instead, there were three scribbled pages of bloc-note paper with some character sketches that weren't going to be much help because the real problem was going to be how to get them all together and have things happen to them. What was 'Sardine' going to say to Madilyn Fishstain (which was the name he'd decided *not* to use for the girl he was copying after Margot, but hadn't yet thought of a replacement)? He'd also a name for a man floating in his mind which he did like – Dr Jellyroll – but couldn't think of a personality to go with it. Who could Dr Jellyroll be?

Then he started thinking of Margot again and suddenly went to the phone and dialed her number – Dr Jellyroll would have to wait a bit longer before achieving an identity.

The clerk at Margot's hotel answered and, after a few minutes, told him that she was out. She must be at Oliver's he thought, that's where she'd said she spent her afternoons. He dialed the number slowly, thinking that if Oliver answered he would adapt as normal a tone as possible and so indicate that what had happened between Oliver and Vivian was a closed incident. He would even make it seem that that was the purpose of his call – to let Oliver know that everything was all right, that he wasn't holding a grudge, and so on . . .

However, it was Margot who answered.

'It's Trent,' he said. 'How's everything?'

'Everything's fine. Where have you been?'

'I've been trying to get started on the book,' he mumbled, hoping she wouldn't start asking a lot of questions. It was embarrassing that he hadn't even written the first page.

'I thought you were coming over to see us.'

He thought he detected a guarded note of desire in her voice. Perhaps his four-day absence had had its effect.

He answered with warmth:

'I was just thinking of coming over now. That's why I phoned. Is Oliver there?'

'Yes. Wait a second, I'll put him on.'

He wondered if he'd have time to quickly remind her to take her panties off in honor of his visit, but it would be too stupid if he found himself telling it to Oliver by mistake.

'Hello, Trent,' Oliver sounded apologetic and as if he were hoping there wasn't going to be a scene.

Trent decided to let him suffer in suspense a little longer and said non-committedly:

'I was wondering if I could drop by in about a half-hour.'

'Certainly. What's on your mind?'

'All right, I'll be over in a little while,' Trent said and hung up.

7

It was shockingly cold when Trent got in the street; much too cold, he thought, to queue up with the huddled group of miserable housewives and wait for a bus. It was six-thirty, and at this hour all the buses were jampacked with the homeward bound workers and housewives of Paris. The buses rushed by without stopping. They were full and the women waited silently for one to come along that had some room. Not one of these women would have thought of taking a cab, although they were all cold, tired, hungry, and angry because the dinner would be late; and the brief hour they had after they cleared their tables, and before they dropped off asleep, the hour when they sat knitting and listening to the radio with the children safely asleep, the best hour, would be shorter than usual – but none would take a taxi. They were thrifty, and had to be. Life on the war-wracked continent had taught them the virtue of self-denial, or the vice of frugality, according to how you looked at it.

At any rate, they thought it would be sinful to take a cab. Cabs were for when you were taken violently sick and couldn't stand up; cabs were ambulances. Ironically, he, Trent, with plenty of money and who thought nothing of taking taxis, couldn't find one, since they too were all taken (by other people with plenty of money). And he started walking to Oliver's, hoping to catch a cab or bus on the way.

It was quite cold – the first winter-like day of the fall – and he hadn't dressed warmly enough.

'Winter in Paris,' he thought. It was a grim spectacle. If the Americans could see what it was like in Paris in the winter then they'd understand why everybody thought the spring was terrific.

He thought of the bums that sleep on the subway grills with a few sheets of newspaper on them on the cold January nights. And the winter was gray and without snow at Paris, and was escorted by an epidemic of grippe, so that both the rich and the poor were coughing and sneezing and staying home with fevers.

He passed another bus-stop with its chorus of tragic women. He tried to read their tired faces and mused at how different his life was from theirs. He respected them; for what they were suffering seemed so much more honest than his own preoccupations. When he thought of what he was up to at the moment – hurrying to Oliver's house and hoping to deceive him there – and of how the women waited patiently in the cold, desiring nothing better than to go home and to sleep, he was struck by how trivial his behavior was . . .

But why was he getting all these ideas about The Winter, and about the groups of melancholy women . . .? He was accustomed to feeling sharp little stings of guilt at the sight of the poor, and he knew very well he didn't like the winter; but he wasn't used to having so many, and such vivid thoughts about them. '"Vivid" isn't the word,' he thought, 'it should be "verbal".' Because his thoughts were coming on as if they were paragraphs printed on paper . . . he felt as if he could almost read them aloud . . .

He had spent four days trying to write and now, perversely, as soon as he had given up trying and left his writing table, his brain had begun to comply, and was producing pages of words like a printing press.

'That's why what I'm doing is trivial,' he thought with grim delight, 'because my brain doesn't work right.' If he was the only one bent on evil in a world of good people on their way home after work, it was because of his own disobedient mind which balked at the worthy endeavors he assigned it, and only came alive when there was sex in the offing . . .

Margot opened the door. She had on a gray skirt and a black turtle-neck sweater, and in the room behind her he could see Oliver getting up and smiling nervously.

'How's Poland?' Oliver said.

Oliver and Trent were in the habit of speaking a great deal about politics. It was practically the basis for their friendship. Both read the newspapers compulsively and immensely enjoyed having someone to discuss it all with. Neither had any fixed position but it was understood that they would argue anyway, automatically opposing each other's viewpoints. Thus they had each been communists, Catholics, Moslems, Negroes, Jews, Italians and yogis, in order to make opposition. This was done in the nicest possible way – just for the pleasures of oratory. Often they were in agreement, moreover, and would smirk and wisecrack about the same thing. When the news of the Polish riots came, and the Hungarian uprising and war of the Suez canal, they had outdone themselves and stayed up entire nights speculating about the events. That was why Oliver said, 'How's Poland?'

Trent nodded his head and said, in a friendly way:

'Fuck you.'

Oliver smiled with relief and replied:

'Now don't go using any of your big words with me . . . just because I never went to college – I can still look them up in a dictionary you know . . .'

He was as pleased as the devil, Trent thought. Truce had been declared: there wasn't going to be a scene. Well, that suited him perfectly. The peace and relaxation of a truce were just the right conditions within which to cultivate his 'friendship' with Margot. He went over and sat on Oliver's bed and observed:

'I understand the Soviet Union.' Then he leaned back on the bed, waiting for an answer, and idly glanced about the room. It was a rather large room and contained practically all the ingredients of a regular apartment. There was a fireplace; a sink in one corner, large enough to serve as a sort of bathtub in which sections of the body could be washed in sequence; a tiny, screened-off kitchenette in another corner; a large, roll-top desk; and books – books everywhere. There was also Margot, sitting in a chair and looking at him the way she had looked at Faustino Perez . . .

Oliver was searching for something in a drawer and wasn't looking at them. Trent looked Margot in the eyes, returning her burning glance. She blushed and lowered her eyes, then immediately looked back again and squirmed slightly in her chair.

Oliver had found what he was looking for – a sheet of paper with hundreds of incomprehensible lines and dots and circles all forming a crude, pyramid-like affair.

'I understand the Soviet Union too,' he announced, and held the sheet of paper up in confirmation.

'Oh Christ, don't you want to hear my idea?' Trent grumbled. 'I said it first you know.'

Oliver looked bored and said:

'All right, what?'

'Well not if it's actually going to put you in physical pain, for Christ sakes . . .'

'It's bad enough that *I* don't get to talk,' Oliver brooded aloud, 'but I have to pretend I'm dying to listen to him . . . All right, please, please, PLEASE explain the Soviet Union!'

'Now you're making a joke out of it,' Trent observed, then added: 'But I'll tell you anyhow – I figured out why Krushchev made that speech attacking Stalin.'

Oliver said nothing and Trent continued. 'China; it's all on account of China. China's a big baby. That's the first time that happened – that there was another *big* communist country. China's so big, that people might even begin to wonder if it shouldn't be the number one communist country – espcially because of Mao Tze Tung. Mao's like a combination of Lenin and Stalin. He did it; he was the one that conquered China, and he's still living. The Russians don't have anyone of that stature. That's why they feel a bit uneasy. Suppose all the foreign communist parties started looking to Mao for leadership. It would make sense: the whole communist society was run by one man at the top – Stalin – and Mao is his logical heir not Krushchev or any . . .'

'. . . like a pyramid,' Olive mumbled. He propped his chin in his palm thoughtfully and seemed to be seriously considering Trent's theory.

Seeing him deeply engrossed, Trent looked at Margot who was still staring at him. He cupped his hand over the fly of his trousers as if a secret gift for her were hidden there. Margot's eyes widened and fixed hungrily between his legs.

Oliver continued to ponder, his eyes staring unseeingly into space. He was getting ready to say something; one could see his well-fleshed jaws beginning to work. Trent removed his cupped hand and revealed an incredible bulge in his trousers at which Margot moved nervously in her chair.

'. . . Yes,' Oliver was saying, 'that's not bad; I hadn't thought of it.'

'Of course not. You never hear anything about any friction between Russia and China about which one gets to make the final decisions. They're very careful not to mention it, but it must exist; one of them's got to give the orders . . .'

'Have you ever had any *bruja*?' Oliver asked getting up.

"What's that?'

'It's Trukish,' Oliver said, taking a bottle off a shelf and pouring a bit in a glass.

It was colorless and poured thickly like syrup. Trent sipped some and smacked his lips. It was a very odd tasting thing.

'Made out of figs,' explained Oliver.

Trent finished the sample and held his glass out for more.

'Aren't we all,' he remarked.

Oliver carefully filled the glass and said:

'It'll stone you too. Wait and see what happens.'

Oliver really was an odd one, Trent thought. On the one hand he was an amateur yogi; refusing to eat meat, and spending long immobile periods sitting cross-legged on the floor; and on the other hand he thought nothing of getting juiced to the gills.

He'd gotten to the point where it was truly impossible for him to eat meat, Trent knew, because it disgusted him so. He thought of it as 'flesh' and would have gagged on it had he taken a mouthful. But if he were eating some brewer's yeast, or some whole-wheat germ, he couldn't get over thinking how pure and good it was, and would gobble huge tablespoons of them. That was why he was so fat – from eating kilos of walnuts and raw cabbage in a state of spiritual ecstasy. And he wasn't 'beefy' fat, but 'cabbagy' fat.

He wasn't reluctant to engage in any sex activity either. He considered himself so superior to the erotic experience – 'mere nervous phenomenon' was what he termed love – that he thought he was in no way imperiled by its dangers. And likewise for alcohol which generated a 'crude, but serviceable trance'.

Money was in a similar category. He claimed not to mind how much, or how little of it he had and refused, in any case, to go out of his way to get it. His mother had a pharmacy in Marseilles and sent him a monthly check; and his girlfriends always seemed to understand and helped out . . .

His success with women stemmed from the apparent contempt he had for money and, especially, sex. He had perfected a style in which he could ignore women so successfully that strange ones – on the subway – would try and catch his eye, would cross and recross their legs, would even rub against him, pressing their breasts against his arm, to get his attention. It wouldn't work either: he would go right on reading his newspaper, completely absorbed, and would move slightly from the breast's soft intrusion as if he weren't even aware of what was touching him.

Had he spent his time in the subway like all the other men, assiduously looking up the ladies' skirts and making obscene appeals with his eyes, they would have thought of him as just a fat swine, but his insularity intrigued them, and he always had a good-looking girlfriend with several possible replacements standing by. It was the opposite of Trent's paying Vivian's way in the world and being slavishly grateful for the pitiful bit of 'love' it purchased for him. And Vivian had reacted like the others; had been intrigued by Oliver . . .

Trent drowned the rest of his *bruja* and his eyes sought Margot's over the rim of his glass.

She hadn't left off staring at him for a moment; it was more than just staring too, her eyes pleaded with him to come and savagely bite the nape of her neck and thrust her dress up, grab at her bare and squirming thighs and ravish her like a rutting bear. Anyone else but Oliver would have noticed it – it seemed *too* obvious to Trent. It might spoil everything he thought. Oliver wasn't supposed to know. Why was she acting as if she wanted to let the cat out of the bag? But still, her recklessness aroused him. It dared him to respond with a recklessness of his own . . .

She was sitting in a low armchair facing him, and Oliver was seated at a table somewhat behind – not very well placed to notice Margot's actions it was true . . .

He looked pointedly at her legs, then in her eyes, and commanded, with a fling of his head, that she should open her knees.

'A penny for your thoughts,' Oliver said.

Trent sat staring dreamily at Margot's slender calves – he could see them pumping the pedals of a bicycle with strong and youthful vigor; or thrashing in the water; or sprawling carelessly as they were now, one leg thrust straight out and the other curled back against the chair, the knees a bit apart; or see her bare legs dangling in the air as if she were being mounted by a lover. He said:

'What do you think about the Suez Canal?'

Oliver frowned. It was clear that he was taking the matter seriously. There was also the fact that he was a bit crocked from taking nips of the *bruja* all day long.

When he thought of the Suez Canal, he pictured a map of it he'd seen in a magazine. Spottd along the map were the half-sunken ships that blocked the way. What did he think of it? He wasn't sure. All he could see was the line on the map with the ships lying across it like little matchsticks. He remembered thinking something about it a few days before – the sort of thing he could say to Trent – but all he could think of was the map.

But he'd been sitting for too long with knitted brows and still not saying anything. It was getting ridiculous. Suddenly he got the impression that it might be physically impossible to say anything even if he could think of something – that his voice mightn't work . . .

'It's very complicated,' he blurted, stalling for time and making sure he could still speak.

'Is that all you've got to say?' said Trent.

Oliver thought hard. Now it felt as if his whole mind might be going blank. It was the *bruja*, he knew. It was very sneaky stuff and you couldn't tell what it was going to do next.

'It might be the thing to make Europe unite,' he managed to say finally.

Trent didn't answer at once. His eyes were locked between Margot's open knees. With his hands he was drawing up an imaginary skirt, and she was following suit. The hem of her grey skirt crept up and up, began to round the curve of her knees – and stopped. He could see where the white flesh of her thighs began above the dark silk of the stockings . . .

He went on staring and said with assurance:

'Never. Not a chance in the world for Europe to unite.'

'They might, you can't tell,' said Oliver.

Trent took his time to answer. He seemed to be

considering his reply carefully, but when he did, surprisingly, it was merely to repeat what he had just said.

'What makes you so sure it couldn't happen?' Oliver said. 'It's getting to the point where if we don't unite we'll disappear and, believe me, a thing like that makes it easier and easier to decide to unite.'

'You say "we",' Trent pointed out wearily, 'but you're not talking like a European, or even like a Frenchman, you're talking like an American. Only an American would wonder why all those two-bit countries don't get together and form one real one. It looks so simple. And, for an American, Europe looks like a single country anyway. But you know damn well what goes on in a Frenchman's head when he thinks of himself being a citizen in the same country as a German – it's just too horrible to take seriously. Uh uh, not after what's happened in the last hundred years. There have been three German invasions of France in that time, and all the logic of French history demands that the damn thing be fought to a finish – until, somehow or other, France licks Germany for good. You're not going to tell a guy like that that OK, all that stuff is over now and is going to be left unresolved, and that the next stage is to combine France and Germany as if they were New Jersey and Pennsylvania. I honestly think a Frenchman *would* rather disappear from the map than see that happen. No, Oliver old boy, when you get right down to it, the French would rather merge with the Russians, or anybody, just so long as it would assure their coming out on top of those krauts . . . May I have a bit more of that fig juice?'

Oliver came forward with the bottle and, with a casual gesture, Margot adjusted her skirt which had gotten a good bit above her knees.

'Why don't you try some, honey?' Oliver said to her as he stood, swaying perceptibly, and filled Trent's glass. It sounded as if he had already asked her several times before Trent's arrival and that she had refused.

'All right,' she consented. 'I'd better do something if I'm going to have to listen to another one of these brilliant conversations.'

Oliver brought her a glass of *bruja* and then went back to where he'd been sitting and refilled his own glass.

'Maybe I am talking like an American,' he said, ignoring Margot's sarcastic remark, 'but you're talking like a Frenchman, and a rather elderly one at that. The young ones – the ones that were kids during the war – they're not as hung up about Germany as you think. They might have a bit of an inferiority complex about the fact that their fathers and their older brothers lost the war, but that's all. And the ones that were born a few years after that aren't even going to have an inferiority complex. All they'll know is what they read in the history books and what they hear from a lot of old fogies like you and I – and you know how much that counts for.'

Trent wasn't listening. He was busily engaged in getting Margot's dress and legs arranged the way they had been before Oliver came to serve them their drinks . . .

Slowly, very slowly, he was raising his trousers, holding them delicately by the crease as if they were a skirt. Occasionally he looked her sharply, almost angrily, in the eye with an expression that brooked no contradiction.

Margot was playing her part to the hilt. Puppet-like, as if her hands were attached to his by invisible wires, she raised her skirt until it was once again well over her knees. He was the brother that she adored with a terrible and forbidden passion: no matter to what hellish sin he led her, she would obey.

'. . . this is an eccentric pyramid,' Oliver was saying. He was holding up the sheet of paper that he'd taken from a drawer a while before. Trent glanced at it for a moment – thousands of dots and squibbled lines forming a sort of triangle.

'Yes,' he murmured, and went back to looking at Margot's white thighs. It was getting quite dark in the room from the starting night, and it was beginning to interfere with his view. Oliver's room was always dark for that matter, since it was low in the building and the small window gave on a narrow court so that the sunlight never entered. Oliver had to keep his lamp lit even in the daytime to combat the obscurity, and when the dim, gray daylight that managed to penetrate began to fade, as was happening now, the whole room was plunged in blackness save for a pool of light on the floor directly beneath the lamp.

This meant that pretty soon Oliver would barely be able to see them, unless he turned on the main light in the ceiling. On the other hand, he, Trent, was going to lose the sight of Margot for the same reason.

This thought put him into a state of mild panic, and without losing another second he imperiously signaled her to spread her legs as far as she could to pull her skirt up even more.

Sitting as she was – in a big easy-chair with its back to Oliver – she was effectively concealed from her lover's sight. At the most, Oliver might have noticed her right foot jutting out a bit oddly as she hastened to comply with Trent's bold desire . . .

But Oliver was too absorbed in explaining his pyramid to notice such an insignificant detail.

'The thing that knocks me out about this,' he said, waving the sheet of paper, 'is that it's an absolutely universal symbol – it stands for anything, anything at all. Name anything; any object, any concept, anything! Do you understand? Take any word in the language . . . it works for everything. Say a word, any word at all. Say the first word that comes into your mind.'

Trent's eyes were popping out of his head and his mouth had gone dry. Margot had done exactly as directed, had pulled her skirt up to her belly and had opened her legs as wide as she could get them – even in that dark and shadowy room it was shockingly clear that she had honored her promise and that, like the heroine of her book, she was wearing no panties at all . . .

'There it is,' Trent thought, and a hush of reverence billowed over his mind. Its beauty shocked him. A man couldn't hope to have it happen more than once in all his life that he would have the power to make the young vagina of a lovely, slender, 18-year-old girl suddenly show itself to him; submit to his piercing, lustful eyes.

It seemed to him that it could be a thing to idolize, like some gorgeous trick of Nature's, come upon unexpectedly . . . a fabulous warm mouth.

Margot's face was crimson during all this. She was doing something that she wanted very much to do. An inexplicable longing had sent her through all the complex maneuvers leading to this moment. Perhaps she sensed how beautiful her sex was to be shown; that it would be a pity if no strange male would ever stare at it with taut hunger. Perhaps she craved to see the magic it could cause: fascinate the man like a good look at death, and have his eyes betray it.

Countless generations of the women she stemmed from must have had the same urge bedevil them in dreams, and woken frightened and ashamed. But suddenly the world had changed: what had been true for her mothers had blasted apart and now the Truth was anywhere. The same idea, kept secret for ages in the part of a woman's mind that she divulges to no one, had finally erupted with Margot who was eighteen and who believed in nothing.

She lifted of her own accord, straining the clean-lined muscles of her thighs in order that the secret should be as completely betrayed as possible.

To Trent, this pale, pink wound between her legs, not yet clothed in the shaggy mane of full womanhood but more than half-revealed by a kind of adolescent fur, was equally a summit, not just for him, but for the eyes of many men before him.

'. . . Give me a word,' Oliver still pleaded. His voice had been creaking endlessly, like a toy that wouldn't run down. It seemed to be coming from very far below as though its owner was calling up from the bottom of an abyss. Trent paid no attention to it. He sat savoring the exquisite spectacle of Margot's displayed vulva. It had gotten so dark in the last few minutes that he sensed, rather than saw it. Deep shadows now obscured Margot almost totally, as they did everything else in the room except for Oliver waving his miraculous 'pyramid' in the dim lamplight.

'A word . . .,' Oliver said again.

'PUSSY!' shouted Trent and, taking a step in the dark, knelt in front of Margot's and solemnly kissed it . . .

He had lost his head obviously, and had moved across the short space that separated him from Margot and was pressing his lips to her hot little spot without knowing very well how he had gotten there. Margot stifled a gasp at the shocking contact of his mouth against her orifice. But she was even more enmeshed in the wild game they had been playing than he, and she arched lasciviously against his face, making no attempt to rebuff him but actually urging him on.

It was Trent that got cold feet and, hurriedly standing up, he said, 'Hey, how about putting the goddamn light on,' as if he had been trying to go somewhere and had stumbled in the dark.

Oliver had noticed nothing and was blissfully expounding his idea, 'There are two ways of looking at "pussy". You can think of it as being everything the term applies to – general "*pussy*", or you can think of some particular "pussy". Either way, the pyramid symbolizes them perfectly.

'Take the first one, the general one. You're dealing with all the pussies in history. Think of them as forming a very distinct group as contrasted with everything else – like the buffaloes for instance, or like all the people who have hunchbacks. In a way, they are at war with everything else: they tend to make all the other things diminish and themselves grow more important. Eventually, they want to conquer the world, just like the ants do, or the germs for diphtheria. It's very much as if they were a living thing. The way they operate is just by being themselves as much as possible . . . "Look at us!" all the pussies in the world are saying together . . . they can't get enough attention . . . they want you to forget about your job, forget about law and order, forget about the stomachs and the hearts, and just think about Pussy. Can't you just hear them talking among themselves on the sidelines, so to speak? Patting each other on the back about the supreme importance of their role in reproduction; nudging themselves in the ribs as one of those situations develops in which the course of human history is altered because of some great man getting a hardon; nodding their heads knowingly at the sight of a young girl being a prostitute for the first time . . .

'Well, all those pussies, taken as a bloc, are in the exact

99

shape of a pyramid. They have the huge base – that's the seething mass of pussydom you might say, and everything that takes place within it has to do with just one thing – Pussy. Pussy this, pussy that, how many pussies are there? What do pussies like? What makes a pussy fall in love? Is taking a swim after a large lunch dangerous for the pussy?

'But the pyramid tapers, getting tinner and thinner, growing more and more compact, forcing up, at the end, a single pussy which is the apex, and which carries the combined thrust of all the countless pussies below in their concerted will to form a sharp tip at the top, and to literally pierce into the non-pussy world and lance it through.

'This brings us to the case of the particular pussy, because any pussy, looked at all alone, is like the final pussy at the apex of the pyramid. It is Jane's pussy, or Betty's pussy, or the pussy of the girl next door. All by itself, it makes a little pyramid of its own, what with its trying to invaginate every cylindrical object in sight. Furthermore, it tries to become the apex of its girl's life – Betty's or Jane's or whatever her name may be – and often succeeds in getting to be the boss of the pyramid of her existence and that of those about her. Furthermore –'

'Oh, shut up for Christ sake!' Margot sounded really furious, and both Trent and Oliver looked at her with surprise. She had a number of reasons for being angry: Oliver had snapped the ceiling light on, flooding the room with light, and had continued his discourse complacently and absolutely oblivious to the fact that she was making a fool of him, and his ridiculous speech about 'pussies' was making a comedy out of the game of make-believe incest that she so much wanted to play with Trent. Oliver was supposed to be their father, and he wasn't supposed to totally ignore their forbidden interest in each other – he was supposed to be a trifle suspicious. He wasn't doing it at all, and it was ruining everything. Unconsciously, she not only wished Oliver to be a trifle suspicious, but wanted him to actually catch them at something. It was a reaction to the maddening detachment he affected in relation to all things sexual – including herself.

Trent thought it astonishing that she should be angry instead of being, as he was, grateful that they hadn't been discovered. He was doubly perplexed because he had imagined, listening to Oliver, that this was the kind of fuzzy monologue that Margot thought was 'brilliant', and which attracted her to him.

'Maybe that *bruja* is too much for you,' said Oliver with a touch of irritation.

'I thought what you were saying was pretty interesting,' Trent said, taking Oliver's part and anxious for him to resume his absorption in pyramids. 'And I liked that when you said that a pussy has girl instead of the other way around.'

'When did I say that?' asked Oliver curiously.

'Well, you didn't use those words exactly, but you said something about each pussy trying to become the apex of its girl's life . . . it's funny to picture a pussy thinking, "my girl's name is Sylvia".'

'Christ! What a conversation!' Margot exploded again.

'I suppose there's a little too much truth in it for comfort,' Oliver suggested nastily.

'Are you suggesting that *my* pussy reminds you of a pyramid? Because if you are – '

'Now, now,' Oliver said with a chuckle, 'there's no need to start getting melodramatic. I certainly didn't mean to cast the slightest reflection on your pussy, darling, I was merely illustrating my point about the pyramid being a universal symbol. I don't even know how "pussy" got into it – oh yes, that was Trent's idea to use "pussy." It would have been much better by the way, if he'd said something like Catholicism or – '

'Before you get started again,' Margot interrupted, 'what are we going to do about supper? It's getting pretty late you know.'

'Make some eggs or something,' Oliver grumped, then, turning to Trent, 'Why don't you stay and have dinner with us?'

'Thanks, I'd like to,' Trent answered.

'Well, in that case, I might as well call Vivian and tell her to come too,' said Margot. 'I'm going to need some-body to talk to if you two are going to start in with your pyramids again.'

She was at the phone and dialing it before either Oliver or Trent could think of something to say to stop her. Instead, they looked at each other, each one wondering how to react to this embarrassing turn of events. After a moment, Oliver got up and silently filled Trent's glass and his own with *bruja*. Then they waited . . .

Things were getting out of hand, Trent thought, as he listened to Margot chatting on the phone to Vivian. He'd been avoiding her for a week and now she was coming here, to Oliver's room which was the last place in the world he wanted to see her. The embarrassment of seeing her with Oliver was coupled with the embarrassment of being in the same room with her and Margot – it was so awkward that it ceased to be a problem, and he emptied his glass and held it out for more . . .

By the time Vivian arrived, he and Oliver had had several more glasses of *bruja* and it was evident that there wasn't going to be the slightest difficulty – as far as the men were concerned at least – in ignoring the rather delicate situation.

'Hi there, old girl,' he gurgled with an asinine grin.

Vivian glared at him furiously. She was as angry as Margot had been a short while before, and for a similar reason. Entering this room, where she was going to be in the presence of Oliver and Trent for the first time since the agonizing moment when the one had suddenly entered and found her making love with the other, she had expected an awkward silence, or an attempt at a casual greeting which would vainly strive to conceal a strong undercurrent of emotions – hate, desire, jealousy . . . There might also be a solemn, almost religious tone of forgiveness. It promised to be very dramatic. The fact that Margot, Oliver's mistress, was there could only heighten the tension. It promised to be one of the most towering scenes of her life – and there was Trent, hopelessly drunk and jabbering like an idiot, and Oliver with the same fatuous leer, looking as if he wouldn't be able to stand up without help!

Trent explained his state of mind spontaneously.

'I don't give a shit if you make that kind of a face.'

Vivian considered, for a moment, whether she shouldn't turn her back on them all and go back out the door, but Margot who, fortunately, had gotten a bit drunk herself, beckoned to her and coaxed:

'Come and talk to me Vivian – these rats have got me outnumbered.' And Oliver, although not able to rise, said, like an amiable cripple:

'Come and pour yourself a glass of *bruja*, Vivian . . . we're hilarious . . . we're many, many *brujas* ahead of thee.'

Vivian allowed herself to become infected with the group's intoxicated mood. She seldom drank, and two

103

glasses of the sirupy juice stung her powerfully. Soon, she had drawn a chair up next to Margot, and the two of them babbled away gaily, and more or less on the verge of having an outright laughing jag.

As for Trent and Oliver, they were paralyzed. From time to time, they could both be heard mumbling things, but it could hardly be called a conversation.

It wasn't an unpleasant thing, this stupor, Trent reflected. In spite of the fact that he had lost control of his limbs, inwardly his mind was as clear as a mountain pool (at times), and could practically be said to be 'alert.'

Things happened . . . he couldn't quite see how they began or ended . . . now and then, he found himself sitting in one or another of the places to sit . . . occasionally, he would realize that he was standing in the tiny toilet that was outside in the hall, in the process of making water . . . once, he had a dish of scrambled eggs on his lap and was eating them with a fork . . .

At present, he sat in the armchair facing the bed. Vivian and Oliver sat on opposite corners of it and, as he watched, Margot came and stretched out on it on her back, and with her head resting in Oliver's lap.

Mechanically, his eyes followed her legs as she arranged herself on the bed. At first she stretched them out straight before her, then, not finding this comfortable, drew her knees up till her high heels were resting on the bedspread . . .

So, the game was going to start again – he was afforded the sight of her bare derriére; of the smooth, white thighs joining in the place where love enters – even though Vivian was present. In her imagination, Margot had no doubt assigned the role of 'mother' to her. It was a beautiful idea too, Trent thought, his eyes weltering in his gorgeous 'sister's' maidenhood.

But Vivian, womanishly, noticed at once and said:

'That's quite a free show Trent's getting, Margot.'

(Dirty bitch, thought Trent indignantly. It was as if she were saying, 'Trent's having fun, somebody,' and, of course, 'somebody' would stop whatever they were doing, since it was understood that Trent wasn't supposed to have any fun.)

'What?' Margot said, pretending not to understand, and not making a move as Trent continued to stare with grim and ostentatious delight at her tufted crack.

'Trent is looking at everything you've got,' Vivian said, raising her voice.

(If she knew that Margot wasn't wearing any underwear, she'd say it still louder, he thought.)

'Oh my God!' Margot cried in mock embarrassment, and brought her legs down quickly as the others, Trent included, emitted a good-natured guffaw.

He wasn't certain who had first brought up the topic of the Art Students' Ball, nor when they decided they were going to go, but, at a certain point, a great deal of bustling commenced. It went on for what seemed like hours, this preparation to depart. It was a masquerade, it seemed, and, laughing hysterically, the two women costumed him and Oliver and then stepped behind a screen that stood in one corner and dressed themselves.

'Bravo!' Oliver screamed when they emerged. Vivian was a hula-hula girl. She wore a real knee-length, grass skirt that Margot had dug up someplace and, over her breasts, had tied a lavender scarf halter-fashion. With her blonde hair and creamy, white stomach, it was a very effective outfit. Trent wondered what she had on under the grass skirt – at every step, her naked thighs were exposed, but it was tantalizingly hard to see what she wore underneath. It was much simpler to see what she was wearing under the halter – nothing. Parts of the silken scarf lay in folds and clothed her breasts properly, but the other parts, where there was just one thickness of the material, were completely transparent and one of her round, red nipples showed. This seemed a bit shocking, but was, Trent knew, nothing unusual for the kind of affair they were going to.

Margot had done little more than make a long slit in her tight, gray skirt and put on a man's cap. With a turquoise garter around the black-silk stocking of her exposed leg, she made an adorable apache. Trent wondered what she had on underneath also, and whether Vivian had noticed that she hadn't been wearing anything when she had been giving him his 'free show.'

As for his costume, he wasn't quite sure what he was supposed to be. He and Oliver were both dressed in old rags, and the girls had drawn flamboyant moustaches on them with charcoal. Perhaps they were supposed to be pirates, he thought, or shipwrecked sailors – not that it made the slightest difference . . .

8

It was insane. There was so much screaming and shouting that it was impossible to speak. The wooden floor sagged and rebounded in time to the mob who were jumping up and down in unison.

It wasn't the ordinary Art Students' Ball; held in some slick auditorium, brilliantly lighted, full of newspaper photographers and tourists: it was some huge, dimly lit, old room – perhaps an abandoned livery stable – reached through a succession of alleys and little doors, in which hundreds of fantastically costumed figures jumped and screamed – some obscure ball smacking of the Black Mass and orgiastic riot.

Trent burst out laughing at the sheer insanity of it all. He had been threading his way with the others across the densely packed place and had become detached. Over a loudspeaker system, a record blared a lively, turn-of-the-century Parisian tune, and Trent began to leap up and down with the others in time to its music.

The floor dipped and sprang back. Trent was a tornado of energy; just before leaving the house, Oliver had distributed benzedrine tablets to counteract the torpor which the *bruja* had induced in all of them and which threatened to render them immobile. As a result, his body now took an active part in his mental follies.

He found himself dancing the mambo with a luscious, Arab belly dancer. Someone had suddenly changed the record, and everyone had begun to dance with the nearest available partner. The girl he danced with wore a veil and

107

silken trousers. Her eyes were like gray, misty pools. They looked into his own and he read so much hot passion there that his head emptied of Vivian, emptied of the demented, screaming mob . . .

Vivian scanned the room looking for Trent. They had managed to traverse the swarming throng, and stood now in a corner of the immense room that was relatively clear. The whole room was being lit by a few scattered lamps and candles. It wasn't nearly enough. The walls and ceiling flashed black with the colossal shadows of the dancers. Her heart beat like a trip hammer as a result of what had happened to her – coming across that room had been like running a gauntlet of sex-starved convicts. Men had stared hungrily at her; mouths had brushed close to her ears, whispering obscenities; and hands – hands coming from everywhere that boldly caressed her, squeezing her breasts and buttocks, and probed their insolent fingers into the grass skirt. There was no escape: as she grasped one hand and pushed it from her breast, where it threatened to rip the frail, silk halter off, another glided expertly between her thighs from behind her . . . found the edge of the brief panties and rapidly slipped under it . . .

All the women in the place were being frisked in a similar manner, but this is not to say that Vivian's entrance hadn't been marked. Many of the women were beautiful – they were artist's models a lot of them, and mistresses of artists – but the men who were close enough to Vivian to make her out in the dim light, immediately approached her, in preference to anyone else they might see, to fondle her legs and belly and breasts. So few blondes are very beautiful that when men see one, it's a well-known fact that they cease paying attention to everyone else. Furthermore, they sensed that Vivian was a foreigner which intrigued them. So even though there were dozens of truly exquisite French girls, like Margot, the males all turned to the blonde, hula hula girl . . .

Oliver spied the bar – a sort of window in the wall not far from them, through which drinks were being handed. He had been standing and regarding the dancers benevolently, and now started off purposefully towards the liquor. Vivian began to follow but Margot caught her by the arm.

'He'll be all right,' she said, looking around the room with a hard glint in her eye. 'Let's see if we can't find somebody to dance with . . .'

Neither of them had forgotten their anger of earlier in the evening when their respective vanities had been punctured. Margot had been furious with Oliver because he'd been so absorbed in what he'd been saying that he hadn't even noticed that Trent was kissing her on the vagina. And Vivian had been more than vexed with Trent for having been rowdy and vulgar when he should have been pensive and despondent. Now, with their men drunk and distracted, Margot was suggesting, they could take their revenge.

The room spun and tottered spasmodically like a wounded carousel. Trent leaned against a wall, feeling as if he ought to hold on to keep from being tumbled to the floor. He closed his eyes and a wave of nausea swept through him. Where the hell was Vivian? he wondered, and, opening his eyes, looked blearily about him. And where was the belly dancer? He remembered her smoldering eyes with a stab of remorse . . . Where had she gotten to?

Adding to the din, a man not far from Trent, dressed as Julius Caesar, began to throw firecrackers into the crowd. One of them landed at Trent's feet and he looked at it as the little fuse sputtered. When it exploded, part of it flew off and hit him in the ankle. It hurt. He let go of the wall reluctantly and slowly fled from the area. This entailed moving out on the dance floor and immediately he bumped into Margot. She was dancing with a very thin Santa Claus whom Trent recognized, after a few moments, as being Ben, the publisher.

'Hi there,' he said, conscious, as drunk as he was, of wanting to make a good impression on Ben. 'I have a well-nigh overwhelming yen to dance. It's been many, many years since I had a yen like that – matter of fact, I never had one, but just now it suddenly hit me.' And, addressing Ben, 'How are you, by the way? How's everything down at the – what shall I say, the firm, the office?'

'Everything's fine. We're all waiting for your book with bated breath.'

'Let's not talk shop; let's dance,' Trent said, executing a few steps by himself and snapping his fingers.

'A man with a one-track mind,' Ben observed, and gallantly handed over Margot.

He took her in his arms and danced off. As soon as they were conveniently concealed in the thickly crowded center of the dance floor, he wrapped both arms about her and pressed her body to his own.

'Now I've got you, you little rascal,' he whispered to her, and kissed her ardently behind the ear.

The sight of her, and the 'feel' of her in his arms had done wonders for the slight attack of nausea and vertigo he'd undergone a short while before. The fact that he was able to dance at all was a small miracle, equivalent to the improvement in morale of a hospital patient to whom a pretty nurse had been assigned.

His hands were locked together behind her, low on her

110

back, and she had raised her arms and clasped her hands behind his neck. It was the way one danced at the 'Bal Négre,' and at the other cheap dance-halls of Paris – places frequented by prostitutes and pimps and the underworld in general. It was the position in which he could feel her belly, and the imprint of her hard young breasts most completely.

'Stop that!' Margot commanded suddenly.

'Stop what?'

She looked over her shoulder quickly. 'Oh, excuse me. Somebody was feeling my ass. I thought it was you.'

'You mean I don't have the right?' he whined in mock dismay. As always, he was absolutely charmed by her vulgarity. He knew that from her way of thinking it was a question of honesty as a writer that made her employ the blunt, Anglo-Saxon terms in her speech, rather than the approved circumlocutions that nice young ladies were supposed to use; but the contrast between the gross words, and the exquisite, delicate creature pronouncing them, made him want to laugh aloud with pleasure.

'Of course you do. We've been introduced, haven't we? It's just that I don't like the idea of complete strangers – '

'Where is he? Where is the filthy cad?' There was a knight in armor, a zombie, and a splendidly-muscled, half-naked African witch doctor, all within easy reach of Margot's provocative rump. Trent spread his hands lovingly over that part of her anatomy to protect it from the unknown assailant. He sighed and gently rubbed and kneaded it, handling it as if it were the most precious thing he had in the world; and the more he caressed it the more his passion mounted, becoming so pronounced that it forced all other states and emotions to diminish – soon he had hardly any room left to be drunk.

Margot was docile. She leaned her breasts against his

111

hard, male chest and danced dreamily, and when after a while, his hand slid down to where the slit parted her tight skirt, she rested her head on his shoulder and closed her eyes.

He allowed his hand to ride on the bare flesh of her thigh for a long time, loving the feeling of it – silken and moving . . . He didn't move his hand into the slit; he simply desired for it to happen and their movements did the rest. The dress opened and swallowed his hand and then, somehow, her thigh worked its way around, inch by inch, and at length the cheeks of her behind were being fondled against his fingers. As usual, she wasn't wearing any underwear. Through the satiny skin he felt the voluptuous play of the muscles of her dancing legs. He spread the fingers of this hand and tried to cover her butt as if she were a baby he was holding in his hand –

'How do you like my ass?' Margot murmured.

All these stimuli had been having their effect on him. His joint had become big and stiff and he had been dancing with his body turned somewhat to the side to avoid touching her with it. Now, in answer to her question, he turned full against her and let her feel his aching erection.

Anyone looking at them could have seen without the slightest effort that he had his hand under her skirt and was palpitating her buttocks – worse than that, the fact that his hand was where it was had forced the skirt to open in a most shocking manner, so that instead of the slit skirt, which only allowed glimpses of the bare flesh of her thigh above her stocking-top, her whole leg was uncovered now and (in profile) her derriere.

This startling spectacle did not receive the attention it would have seemed to merit for the simple reason that almost every other couple dancing were being equally lascivious, and there were sights more shocking than half of a girl's bottom with a man's hand stroking it. One pair of eyes, however, was fastened on Margot and Trent, and was noting their behavior with utmost interest . . .

'Take it off!' This terse command emanated from a man dressed as Sherlock Holmes and was directed at Vivian. He had walked up to her determinedly and expressed his will like an army officer. Vivian shot him an icy glance and then went back to the incredible sight of Trent giving Margot tender little kisses as they danced, and ostentatiously stroking and squeezing her uncovered rump. She'd been watching them for a long time, convincing herself that her eyes weren't playing tricks on her, and speculating rapidly as to what sort of reaction was called for.

'Strip! Let's go! Take it off, God damn it!' Sherlock Holmes barked. He seemed not able to understand why she was taking so long, and was getting angrier by the minute. It was making her nervous. She decided not to look at him this time – ignoring him would be the quickest way to get rid of him. 'All right, I'll count to ten,' he said. He's a real maniac, she thought, and knew automatically that he would pronounce the numbers like a telephone operator . . . 'Wah-un, tew-wu, tha-ree . . .' He didn't bother to count any further but casually reached over and jerked the flimsy, silken halter off.

'Give it back!' she gasped, stooping over and covering her nipples and as much of her breasts as possible with her hands. She was very close to bursting into tears.

'What a lovely pair of tits you've got there! Why it's a sin to keep them all covered up like that.' He was contemplating his handiwork contentedly and seemed to be getting ready to rip off the grass skirt.

'Give it *back!*' She was pleading now – unashamedly.

113

She had the impression that nobody was paying attention to what was happening to her. This would have been quite possible given the nature of art-students' dances in general, and this one in particular. Anyone who saw Sherlock Holmes snatch the purple scarf from Vivian's bosom would have thought it a raucous bit of horse-play, which, no doubt, was all it was, but someone *was* watching – the African witch doctor – and he had noticed that Vivian was on the verge of hysterics.

'Mimimimimimimi,' bleated Sherlock Holmes, mocking her voice which had sounded as if it might degenerate into blubbering. At the same time, he noticed that the witch doctor was observing the comical little scene, and flashed him a wink of connivance.

The witch doctor took a step forward. 'Why don't you give it back, man?' He said it softly and reasonably. His muscles were superb, and he was frowning a little.

Sherlock Holmes briefly appraised this new element in the situation, made a few deductions and replied:

'I was just about to do that very thing.' He offered the scarf to Vivian, smiling like a good sport and peeping at the round, pink nipple she exposed as she reached out to take it.

Oliver danced very slowly, paying no attention whatsoever to the music. He was doing very well, considering the amount of alcohol in him, and probably could have kept time with the *paso doble* that was being played, but, for what he was doing to the big redhead in his arms, he preferred to have as little unnecessary forward motion as possible. They were almost stationary as a matter of fact, but in compensation for his absence of linear progress, Oliver's whole body – from the feet up – was performing a stupendous repertoire of squirms, wriggles, diddles and bumps. He was, as the expression used to go, 'socking it in'.

As for the redhead, she accepted this buffeting with a straight face, but a film of sweat on her forehead and a pink blush on her features indicated that Oliver had stoked up her passion to the melting point. He knew her slightly – her name was Lila and she worked for Ben, Margot's publisher – but none of the details of her personality held any interest for him. All he knew was that she was big and voluptuous, was dressed like a vamp of the 1920s and had flaming red hair.

He performed his dance, which consisted of rubbing, pressing, and butting every part of his anatomy against every part of her, with great concentration, and wasn't aware that Trent and Margot were dancing a few feet away. Nor were they, at first, although Trent did notice Lila because of her hair and the fact that her dress, covered with sequins, was flashing to a remarkable extent due to the pounding of Oliver's body. This intrigued Trent and he maneuvered Margot till the two women were back to back at which point he reached out to feel Lila's violently trembling buttocks. This sort of thing had been occurring to her so frequently that she didn't bother to turn around, but Trent suddenly noticed that her partner was Oliver – pumping away with closed eyes – and hastily left off carressing Lila and tried to dance away before Margot saw Oliver. He was afraid this might interfere with his plan, which was to get Margot off into some quiet corner for ten or fifteen minutes and satisfy his long-frustrated desire. The dancing had heated him to fever-pitch and he trusted that it had done the same for Margot. Seeing Oliver, moreover, had reminded him of how little time he had.

'Listen,' he said, 'how about exploring this place? It's a

115

very old house: there must be all kinds of funny little rooms.' Margot had been unusually silent all the time he had been dancing with her and he wasn't sure what she was thinking. She hadn't objected to any of the liberties he'd been taking, at any rate, and for all he knew, he told himself, she might be wondering what was taking him so long to suggest going off and seeking a bit of privacy.

She didn't answer and, a little desperately, he hugged her closely, rubbing his cheek against hers and licking at the lobe of her ear. 'Come on, baby,' he whispered, forcing his hard member against her, 'let's do it. I'm going nuts, I want to do it so bad.' He accompanied his words with his hips in a subtle imitation of the movements of copulation.

Margot wasn't listening to what he was saying. Over his shoulder she was staring at a spot on the dance floor ten yards away at Oliver working on the redhead in a paroxysm of excitement. Both he and Lila looked like they were close to achieving a climax right there in the crowd. Margot's eyes danced with hate. She seemed as if she were about to hiss and spit like an enraged cat.

'You're so beautiful. God, I want to get into you so much! Can't you feel it? Let's make it. Let's get the hell out of here. Nobody's going to notice. Do you want to? OK?' Trent was carried way with desire. He had danced to the edge of the floor and now took her arm and headed for a dim hallway through which he had noticed some amorous couples disappear from time to time. He no longer cared if she responded or not; the important thing was to get her out of there, to get her someplace where it was dark and they would be alone . . .

'Excuse me a minute,' said Margot, freeing her arm. 'I have to go to the john.'

She walked away swiftly leaving Trent disconcerted and

116

alone. He waited impatiently for her to return and, to pass the time, inspected the amazing conglomeration of costumes, particularly those of the women, nearly all of which were designed to present their wearers in a state of semi-nudity. Vivian's costume and Margot's tended to be conservative compared with some of the others. One willowly blonde, for example, seemed at first to be dressed in an ordinary if somewhat expensive style, wearing a strapless chiffon gown; but a closer inspection revealed a curious detail: the dress had a hole – about two square inches big – over her right breast, out of which innocently protruded the plump little bud of her nipple. Similarly, several of the dresses were cut low in the back; so low, that the beginning of the crack of the rump was visible. Moreover, a few of the women had carried this 'peep hole' fashion to its logical extreme and had cut subtle openings in their dresses so that an inquisitive finger, on entering, would touch precisely on the clitoris.

Sights such as these weren't calculated to take Trent's mind off his goal and he searched more and more anxiously in the crowd for the returning Margot. Many minutes went by and his impatience began to turn into wrath at the idea that perhaps she wasn't coming back. Suddenly, he saw something which made him even angrier: there was a powerful African, dressed in a costume of barbaric splendor – ostrich plumes, leopard pelt, massive, brass bracelets – he'd seen him before, he remembered, only this time he was dancing with Vivian!

He'd almost forgotten that Vivian was there, he'd been so preoccupied with Margot, but Vivian *was* there; very much so he noted, coiling slowly around with a man's chocolate-colored bare thigh planted solidly between her legs and half lost in the swirling, grass skirt. He wondered if the African mightn't be exploring her body with his hands. It wouldn't be like Vivian to let him do a thing like that; still, what the hell was she doing dancing with him in the first place? He considered going over and breaking it up; Vivian had never looked more exquisite and the thought that she might be allowing herself to be manhandled caused a sharp stab of dread to race through him. No, he decided finally, first he was going to settle his account with Margot, he was too close to achieving his desire to quit now . . .

He worked his way through the crowd and took up a position near the door of the ladies' room so as to be sure not to miss Margot when she came out. He stood there for about five minutes. It was clear that Margot had already come out, or that she had never gone in; but not knowing what else to do, and numb with disappointment, he remained at his post. After a few more minutes, the door opened and out stepped a delicious cancan dancer. She took a few steps and then paused, not far from Trent, as if she too were waiting for someone.

She was very small and doll-like with glossy, black hair and highly rouged cheeks. Looking at her made Trent feel a bit better and, automatically, he began to associate himself with her and cease to worry about Margot and Vivian.

She seemed to be pouting – maybe she was angry about something – or maybe she had one of those mouths like so many French girls that pout perpetually. It was a sign of great sexiness, Trent told himself, girls with that kind of mouth, especially the doll-like type, were the dirtiest females of all. They pouted because they weren't getting laid enough. They could never get laid enough; and even while they were getting laid they went on pouting because it wasn't dirty enough to suit them. They were the easiest type of woman to make too, because they were so

118

insatiable and because they were likely to give just about anybody a chance in their endless search for the magic dick of their dreams.

She caught him looking at her legs, which were adorable in their black-silk stockings with lavender garters, and her lips pouted out even more in recognition of the fact that there was a male in the offing.

With a start, Trent realized that he knew her – it was Jacky, Ben's secretary. Apparently, she hadn't recognized him. That was a matter of small importance and Trent started over to her, getting an opening remark prepared and licking his chops in anticipation of what a pungent little dish she was going to be . . .

She seemed to be smiling at him as he approached but as he started to speak, he realized that the smile was addressed over his shoulder to somebody else, and, turning around, he beheld a large cossack – evidently the party she had been waiting for – who thundered between them and snatched the little cancan girl up like a fumbled football.

This was too much. Trent wheeled and headed for the dance floor. He wasn't sure what he was going to do but he felt very much like raping somebody or smacking somebody – Oliver preferably, but almost anybody would do.

Then he ran into the Arab belly dancer that he had danced with when he first arrived.

In a matter of seconds he was dancing with her in the lewdest manner imaginable. Reckless, and libidinous, he rubbed his body against hers as if he were possessed of some incurable itch – and she answered in kind, furnishing a counter-heat which further inflamed his own.

Watching the unimaginable contortions of her abodomen, during a moment when she had broken away and stood wiggling a few feet from him, he decided that it was no mere costume she was wearing, and that she must be an authentic Arab dancer.

Roughly, he pulled her back again and danced slowly, holding her firmly and staring into her magnificent gray eyes. His hands gripped her buttocks boldly, working her back and forth against his loins, and then he felt her hand which had come between his legs and was exploring and measuring the full length of his masculinity.

That did it. Grasping her by the arm he hurried off the floor and headed down the hallway down which he'd planned to flee with Margot previously. It brought them to a flight of stairs leading down to what appeared to be a dingy and faintly-lit cellar.

Someone had considerately covered the floor with straw he noted, and the place would have been ideal except that there were already several couples lying supine and rolling suspiciously in the darker corners. However, there were other rooms in the cellar and he explored them quickly with her. Some of the couples they saw were actually in the act of coitus – not caring, apparently, whether they were seen or not; and he couldn't help noticing that one of the couples was Oliver and Margot. She had searched him out then, not being able to abide the sight of him making love to the big redhead on the dance floor. At any rate, there it was again – the large ass of Oliver pumping masterfully and smugly in time to Margot's groans of delight . . .

Trent didn't care. He hurried till he'd found an isolated nook and practically threw the Arab girl to the ground. He dropped to his knees behind her and hugged her close to him, at the same time easing her to the floor on her back. He tore the veil off quickly and went to kiss her on the lips but she turned her head quickly, as if wanting to get it out of the light. The thought that this might be due to some form of Moslem shyness flashed through Trent's mind as he took her by the chin and turned her face back in the light. Then he ceased everything and stared with astonishment. There was something terribly familiar about the face, and yet, for some reason, he couldn't place it . . . and then, all at once he could – staring up at him, the gray eyes pleading mutely, and minus the pointed, shiny little moustache, was Faustino Perez.

9

'Oliver doesn't know you came to meet me?'

'No. Of course not. You didn't tell Vivian, did you?'

He didn't answer but went over to one of the rowing machines and sat down on the sliding seat. They were in the American Club. It was a Sunday morning and the place was empty. The old concierge had let them in and he had given her a cock and bull story about them being students and needing to use the library. After she had gone they had sneaked down to the gymnasium which was in the basement.

Margot looked for a place to sit, finally chose a wrestling mat, and then said hesitantly:

'Listen, there's something I ought to tell you. I came over here today because you said it was very important, but I almost didn't come and I'm pretty sure I won't do it again after this.'

He looked at the full sweep of her hips and thighs, and her breasts – ripe, quivering mounds. She had on a yellow sweater and a black gabardine skirt. 'Why not?' he said.

'Because of Oliver. After all, I *am* making it with him. It isn't really fair for me to be seeing other men: it cheapens our relationship.'

So that was it, he thought – Oliver. And she wasn't worried for a second about being 'unfair' to him. No, what she was worried about was how he might take his revenge. After seeing the way he was tearing into the redhead on the night of the art students' ball, she had suddenly decided that it wasn't such a good idea after all

122

for her to be seen running around with other men – 'it cheapened her relationship' with Oliver. And where did that leave him? Out in the cold as usual with a lot of memories of her showing him her pussy and letting him feel her ass . . .

'What was it that you wanted to see me about so urgently?' she said, noticing that he looked a bit sullen.

'About my book. I'm having a hell of a time getting started. I had no idea it was going to be so hard to do. If I could just get started I think I'd be all right, but it's like you said, I need some material, I've got to have a real experience to refer to. I can't just start with nothing at all.'

There was a good deal of truth in what he said. She couldn't fail to recognize it. It had been her theory, after all, that writers should experience the things they dealt with, and hadn't he been accommodating enough to play the part of her brother so that she would have a living model to draw from in her incest novel? Elementary justice dictated that she should return the favor.

She got up and walked around a bit nervously, looking at the curious athletic equipment that crowded the little gym – punching bags, parallel bars, weights, strange apparatuses consisting of ropes and pulleys, a monkey bar which was about ten feet high and whose square framework contined innumerable iron tubes, medicine balls . . . 'What's the problem?' she said. 'What's the situation you want to start the book with?'

'Well, you know the general idea – it's about this scientist that's doing research for Kinsey in Greenwich Village. The book has got to be full of all kinds of freaks and people with strange sex habits. My idea was to start right off with some action, get it going at a fast pace, if you know what I mean.'

Margot nodded her head in agreement.

'Okay, so I've got this character named Dr Jellyroll. He's a weirdy. His bit is that he likes to tie chicks up – you know, ropes, and all that.'

'How does he get them to do it?'

'I don't know. He pays them I guess, or he finds chicks that are hard up and lends them money. After that, they're kind of obligated to him and so they let him tie them up because he's been so nice to them . . . Anyway, I thought that might be a good thing to begin that book with.'

'Is that what you want to do, tie me up?' Margot asked.

'Well, if it's all right with you. And while I'm doing it I'm going to try and dig it as a kind of sex thing, if you know what I mean, so that afterwards I'll be able to describe my emotions and all that.'

'Okay,' Margot said with a let's-get-it-over-with attitude. 'Where do you want to do it?'

He got up, feeling a bit silly, and pointed to the monkey bar. 'Over there I guess.'

There were half a dozen skip-ropes hanging on a hook on the wall. He took all of them and went over to the monkey bar. Margot was there, her elbow resting on one of the iron pipes, waiting for instructions.

'Climb up in the inside,' he ordered, and she stooped under the outer bars and then began to climb up after her carrying the ropes. He halted her when she was exactly in the middle and, one by one, fastened her wrists, raising each arm and pulling it straight as he did so, making her firm, young breasts strain hard against the yellow sweater. He was strongly tempted to place his palms on those inviting orbs – but it wasn't yet the moment.

He hung the extra skip-ropes on an adjacent bar and climbed down to the floor where he could better survey the result of his efforts. Margot looked very much like a hapless victim snared in the toils of a great spiderweb. Up till now he had gone about the business of getting her to climb into the web and attaching her there, in an impersonal fashion, as if he were perfoming a necessary but slightly troublesome labor. Now he realized that she actually was helpless and at his mercy: she'd stay there till he got good and ready to untie her and let her down – she'd stay there no matter what he said, or did to her . . .

He crawled back under the monkey bar, stood directly beneath her and looked up. The rungs she stood on were two feet apart and her legs were opened considerably as a result. It was a thing he'd often had fantasies about – to be able to stand directly underneath a girl, a pretty girl with very pretty legs. It came from the frustration of passing thousands of good-looking women in the streets and seeing just enough of their legs beneath their skirts to want to drop down full-length on the sidewalk and look up and see the rest – the white flesh above the tops of the silk stockings, and the roundness of their buttocks and dark patch of their pubic hair outlined against the thin fabric of their panties. All of these parts of Margot were superior examples of their kind: her legs were lithe and the skin like ivory; they terminated in a rump that was a flaring miracle, and, just between them, he could see the small protuberance her mound of Venus made against her underwear.

Suddenly she realized what he was up to and quickly brought her feet together on the same rung.

'I see you've taken to wearing panties,' he said laconically, climbing up next to her.

She gave him a dirty look. 'If I thought you were going to do that I wouldn't have let you do this to me.'

'That's funny. You didn't used to mind . . . you even

125

showed it to me yourself not so long ago, remember? . . .'

'It was a mistake,' Margot muttered. 'And anyhow, you were wrong if you thought it meant anything.'

He didn't answer. He was getting quite angry. So now you've changed your mind, he thought, his hands toying with one of the spare ropes. You sat there that night and showed me your slit and acted like you didn't care if I screwed you right there in front of your boy-friend, and now it turns out that I was 'wrong' if I thought a little thing like that could have meant anything . . . And he remembered how, at the dance, she had ditched him just when they finally had the chance to sneak off and make love. This made him still angrier.

She shifted her weight impatiently, putting one foot on a higher rung. 'Is this going to take much longer?'

He bent down, casually looped the rope about the ankle she had just raised and took a turn around the rung next to it. 'I'm just beginning,' he answered.

'I don't want you to tie my feet,' said Margot. She was beginning to realize that she had put herself in a rather awkward set of circumstances and was getting a little nervous. 'Untie my foot,' she repeated severely.

He descended till he was level with her foot, then, instead of untying it, swiftly looped a rope around her other ankle and bound it firmly in place. 'You know – there *is* something pretty sexy about this,' he said, and carefully placed the palms of his hands on her straining breasts. They were wonderfully resilient; he pressed them a bit harder and his fingertips slowly curled until each hand cupped and squeezed one of her firm and helpless breasts.

'If this is one of your practical jokes – '

'Oh,' he said, ignoring her, 'now that your legs are

126

open again I think I'll go down and have another look.'
Her feet were further apart than before, and the fact that
one was placed higher than the other increased the
exposure of the secret zone between her legs still more.
'It's great . . . I can even see some of your pussy hairs
. . . they're peeping out the edge of your panties,' he
reported enthusiastically from below.

'Untie me! I mean it this time.'

He climbed up. 'Okay – but give me a kiss first,' and he
went to kiss her but she jerked her head away.

'I'm telling you now – take the ropes off.' She said it
softly, like a gangster, hardly moving her lips. It sounded
very dangerous.

He said, 'You know, I think I'll take off your panties
and then go down and have another look – it ought to be
terrific.' He lifted the black gabardine skirt and reached
under it . . . Then she opened her mouth . . .

He'd been waiting for it; it was inevitable – he clapped
one hand over her mouth (the scream never got started),
and whipped out his handkerchief with the other. 'I don't
suppose anything would happen anyway,' he said, gagging
her, 'the concierge is hard of hearing and this place has
exceptionally thick walls, and nobody ever comes here on
Sunday morning – but we mustn't take any chances, must
we?' He regarded her calmly; she was tugging at her
bonds, her eyes burning furiously, and, his own eyes
coldly staring back, he reached under her skirt again and
caught hold of her panties which he ripped open with one,
vicious wrench.

Once again he stood below her and gazed up. He took
his time, even lit a cigarette, and then, taking a draw,
blew the smoke up at Margot's writhing bottom as he
contemplated the girlish crack nestling in its fur – so
young that the hair had still not grown in fully and the

labia were fully revealed. It was strange, he reflected, how much he'd had the opportunity to stare at those few forbidden inches – beginning with the night in the fog when she had so astounded him by pulling the edge of her panties open – and then, mockingly, letting it snap shut again; and then the night in Oliver's room when she had raised her dress and revealed it again, as much as possible in the shadowy light – but then it had been a question of her showing it to him, whereas now it was he who had uncovered it, against her will, and this time it wasn't going to be up to her how long he might look, or whether he mightn't do more than simply look. It was a big difference.

When he'd gotten his fill of devouring it with his eyes – he took so long that he was certain he had it memorized for the rest of his life – he began to mount up towards it. Rung by rung, closer and closer, he went up slowly and respectfully like someone arriving at the summit of a proud mountain. After a while his head was between her feet, and now, as he closed the final gap, he raised her skirt high over his head, bunched it around her waist and tucked it behind the wide leather belt she was wearing. Now, from her belly to her feet, her clothing consisted of her garter belt and stockings, and that was all, and he was rubbing his cheek high on the inside of her thigh as he traveled the last few inches . . .

When he was so close that she could feel the hot breath from his mouth on her maiden spot, he paused. She ceased her wriggling at this moment; her efforts had been futile; the ropes were much too strong, the knots far too tight. Except for several involuntary tremors she held quite still, waiting, wondering what he was going to do. When it happened, her whole body jerked spasmodically and she uttered a muffled, choking screech – with the extreme tip of his tongue he had flicked her precisely at the very center of her orifice. It had been as if a sharply pointed flame had pricked her. A split second later and his entire mouth hungrily, and brutally asaulted her soft vulva. Simultaneously, she was chewed, licked, sucked, nibbled and gourmandized. Tears spurting from her eyes, her mind passed swiftly through the various degrees of hysteria and then blew wide open in a state of authentic insanity.

This outrageous pillage ceased as suddenly as it had begun. He climbed up now so as to be face to face with her. Margot hung limply in her ropes. All recognition of her present predicament had been chased from her mind by a colossal craving; she had to be loved at once – by a penis.

'PENIS! PENIS! PENIS!' throbbed in her head; the letters flashed before her eyes and the sound lived in her ears, only it was more a feeling than a sound: 'PE' was knobbed and smooth and fingered its way into her soul, and 'NIS' was when it pulled out, drawing her soul and her years and the marrow of her bones; *everything;* out of her hole.

Now the turbulent manipulation commenced again; the reprieve had been brief. This time it was his hand's riotous fingers that played havoc with her pudendum. She was so far gone that she no longer felt the difference between when she was being handled and when her pouch was being let alone; it was all one; the hot waves went right on surging through her no matter what happened.

'Oh, there's something I forgot to mention; something about Dr Jellyroll.' For some reason he spoke to her as if she had her wits about her, whereas it was obvious that she had blown her stack completely. 'I forgot to tell you what he does *after* he's got the girl all tied up and helpless . . .

Very deliberately he opened his fly and let his hard cock leap out into the world.

'PENIS!' Margot was in seventh heaven after this spectacular entrance. The Slayer had come into the arena; soon the blinding corrida would begin!

'Do you know what it means to show your twat to a man? Did you think you could do that and then cop out afterwards? Changed your mind . . . Huh? A big mistake . . . was it? Just a little innocent cock teasing . . . Is that it? You were going to cold cock me . . . Right?' All this time he was brandishing his cudgel and getting into position.

She had no idea what he was talking about; she had the smell of man balls burning her nostrils and couldn't wait to be hoisted on that fleshy prong. 'Ahhh!' She grunted with pleasure like an animal – it had begun. One moment she was sagging, moaning, empty; and the next, the rod had penetrated her and her arching body grew tense like a filled out sail. One moment she was still, and the next she was in the midst of a plunging, pounding stampede. The thing that was joined with her was like a snared beast thrashing to be free.

She answered with a fervor that took him by surprise; her hips and buttocks circled and bucked back at him in a squirming frenzy. He yanked her sweater and brassiere up around her neck; her breasts danced like crazy whirlpools before his eyes. Her head flopped this way and that as if her neck were broken.

If he had taken her gag off now he would have heard an endless torrent of the most appalling obscenities conceivable – she shouted them punctuating each lustful thrust of her belly with the dirtiest word she could think

130

of. She was insatiable, wanting to rub herself to ecstasy on the maddening rod within her; wanting there to be the friction of more erections – in her anus, in her mouth, sliding against her face and arms, spurting hot, white jets of spunk on her lips and breasts . . .

He sunk his hands in the cheeks of her rump and they swiveled on his rigid phallus provoking such a sweet agony of pleaure that he wanted to cry out. For a fraction of a second, he thought of Vivian and felt pure pity for her in this huge lust which she would never know, for this supreme ecstasy which she was missing . . . then her image was obliterated from his mind because he fancied he was coming.

It was still a long way off; was simply a faint glow, and was all but quenched by the dazzling shower of sensation that he was experiencing. But it had a certain quality which set it apart. He had never before been aware of an orgasm in such an early phase of its development, or maybe it was because he'd never had an orgasm before that came so profoundly from his soul. In any event, it took an incredibly long time building up and he watched it, fascinated.

At first, in spite of the frantic pace of their lovemaking, it hardly seemed to grow. But suddenly Margot's churning hips and belly, driving at him from every conceivable angle, began to rotate with a new purposefulness and intensity.

'. . . chouffaphruuphuckt,' she gurgled – she too had gotten the signal.

Now it began to increase in both of them; each smack of their bodies swelled it like balloon, raised it like a tower. Each plunge stoked the heat in their loins and, gradually, all their various voluptuous sensations disappeared and were absorbed in the one feeling of the burgeoning orgasm.

Margot thrust at him carefully so that the stiff rod traveling in and out of her would ram far, far into her sheath, filling it, rubbing the soft and sensitive skin for its entire length.

'Here we go,' he panted. '. . . make it, baby . . . Oh, do it! Do it to me! . . .'

She managed to make him penetrate still deeper, engulfing his joint greedily in her torrid hole.

'. . . shake your ass, you bitch! . . . Fuck me! . . .'

'. . . fhrurt! fhrurt! fhrurt!' she moaned, and jammed herself against him as if she wanted to enter into his skin.

He held on tightly to the bars around him to keep from being knocked off to the ground. They were very close to the climax. Something in him had begun to throb with a heavy beat. He felt as if his heart was going to melt and flow into her in hot spasmodic jets. It seemed as if it couldn't possibly take more than a few seconds – the top-heavy tower was about to topple; the ballon was swollen to the bursting point . . . Together they rocked in the final throes of love . . . Margot swung her buttocks back and forth in the last, slow sweeping circles that set the match to the explosion . . . There came an ultimate, unspeakable instant, and then –

Trent put the pen down hastily and whipped out his handkerchief – it was just in time. He sneezed noisily and everybody at the café terrace turned their heads in his direction.

It broke his train of thought. When he turned again to the black notebook he wasn't sure what to write after 'and then'. He'd already described the orgasm in terms of a balloon, a tower and an explosion. Maybe he should combine them all now to tie the thing up . . . something like, 'the glowing tower crumbled with an explosion like the bursting of an immense balloon.'

His mind refused to function. Actually, he was tired of writing – he'd filled quite a few pages of the notebook, he noted with satisfaction. It didn't seem to have very much to do with the idea he had for his book, but he was sure it would fit in someplace. He felt rather wistful too; writing about raping Margot was a pretty feeble substitute for the real thing. Sadly, he paid the waiter and got up and went away.

10

Trent was in a bad way. Something horrible was happening to him. He was sitting and numbly looking at something, and what he was looking at had given him the shock of his life. It was doing something to his brain; disrupting its equilibrium, throwing everything into a crazy turmoil; and the most terrifying thing about it was that he realized it and was powerless to do anything about it.

Ever since the morning when he had opened the door and found Oliver making love to Vivian his life had taken a strange turn – his queer relationship with Margot, his sudden decision to write a book and the unprecedented effect this had had on his personality – things had become increasingly bizarre. Most of all, there had been the insane Art Students' Ball, with its temptations, frustrations and final, lunatic climax when he had discovered that the veiled 'Arab dancing-girl' whom he had become infatuated with, and was about to passionately make love to, was none other than Faustino Perez. But now, something which capped all these events, and made them seem trivial and sane by comparison, had occurred; and this time there was a real danger that his mind would no longer be able to cope with the grotesque thing he was contemplating . . .

It had been more than a week since he had sat at the café table and written his fantasy of raping Margot in the gymnasium of the American Club on a quiet Sunday morning. He had spent the ensuing time in a concerted effort to organize his ideas and make a careful, overall plan for the book he was going to write. This had involved much writing in the black notebook which had begun to have a good number of its pages covered with scribble. It made him feel good to think that he was, at last, 'writing.' It was the one part of his life that was giving him a bit of satisfaction, and the only one, therefore, that contributed to his stability. Had he taken the trouble to look at his work so far objectively, he would have seen that the book itself was still on page zero. Aside from the passage about raping Margot in the American Club that is, which was also the only legible thing, having been written by pen, which was an instrument he used more carefully than pencils for some reason. All the rest of his work consisted of illegible sketches, incomprehensible outlines, obscure observations, and impractical synopses. It was possible that he himself could not read some of the writing or remember what some of the abstruse symbols referred to. At any rate it was an amazing collection of notes containing everything he had been able to think of which he judged might be of use to him in writing his book. There were lists of phrases such as : 'paroxysm of craving', 'passionate frenzy', 'spasm of ecstasy', 'agony of fervor', and 'surging whirlpool of delirium'. And lists of words: 'licentious', 'depraved', 'libidinous', 'lustful', 'lewd', (it was remarkable, he thought, how many began with 'l'), 'lascivious', 'voluptuous', 'lecherous', 'concupiscent', and 'hot'. Here and there were briefly noted ideas for possible incidents in his story: 'jack off in the tiny white hat'; 'nude on a tombstone'; 'girl in a foreign drugstore trying to get a tube of vaginal jelly using sign language'; 'man from Mars – a ball of bristling cocks'; scholarly references: 'taschunt and thabuscht = vagina and penis in Kabyl'; and quotations: 'I'm out to f. every woman in the world and tonight your number's up', 'I got half a brute on just from touching her in the asshole'.

It was hard to see how he expected to integrate this disparate material, or how he was going to choose which of the numerous synopses and rough drafts he would work from. He himself had been avoiding this delicate question, and, for the time being, was content to go on collecting notes and having the illusion that he was thereby accomplishing the job of writing his book, and this was, perhaps, not entirely unjustified, since a certain amount of this sort of thing takes place with most books.

This, in any event, was the sort of thing that had been occupying his mind for the last few days and right up till the moment when the old woman rang the doorbell.

She handed him a lady's pocketbook which, she said, she had found in the Luxembourg Gardens. She'd found the owner's address in the papers that it contained, and had come immediately to return it. It was seldom a week went by that Vivian didn't lose something or other and so Trent wasn't the least bit surprised. He had often wondered how it was possible for Vivian to lose so many objects. It came, he guessed, from the fact that she had 'other things on her mind,' although what those 'things' could be he couldn't imagine, since he himself hardly ever lost anything.

He thanked the woman and tried to give her a reward which she adamantly refused. It was certainly an example of rare honesty, he had thought; he knew he himself would have been incapable of it. After the old woman had left, he had opened the bag to verify its contents. Aside from the predictable jumble of lipsticks, bobby pins, match-books, scraps of paper and the like, there had been a book with a lavender cover which he had taken out and idly opened . . .

136

It was a rather fat little book and its thin pages were covered from top to bottom with Vivian's tiny, careful script. He had skimmed through it, at first casually, then all at once had become rooted to the spot. He stared at the passage that had caught his attention for fully three minutes, then incredulously had begun opening the book at random and slowly reading whatever he had turned to; finally he had drawn up a chair to a table in the parlor and had sat down limp and dumbfounded.

It was a sort of diary – this he had gathered at once – or, more properly speaking, a journal, and dealt exclusively with an aspect of Vivian and part of her life that was so astounding and unsuspected and evil, that he went pale to read it. She wasn't home at the time and, in the completely silent apartment, it seeemed to him that he could hear the excited thumping of his own heart.

This is the sort of thing he was reading:

'. . . under his nose, and told him I did it because I wanted to find out how to screw – for his sake, because he wanted to screw me so much, and because I was so "frigid" – only I was too shy to let him know about it . . . so I screwed Oliver! – a little "surprise" I'd been planning for him, like a birthday present, and everything had gotten all mixed up and must have looked *terrible* to him. Of course, he believed every syllable – God! his conceit is so much greater than mine – . (And they say women are vainer than men!) It was wild when I was laying there with Oliver . . . making it . . . and the door opened and there was Trent's head! . . .'

As he read it, the scene came vividly to life for him. He even remembered how it had felt when he thought he was being suspicious for nothing – a split-second before he opened the door. Then he saw them again, saw Vivian getting 'trimmed;' saw what he had never seen in his life – what a woman looks like with a man on top of her – and have that woman be Vivian. Now he knew what went on in her head at that moment. And he was the one that had gotten stage fright; he remembered the asinine smirk he had had, and how it had felt like a bitter stain on his face. He relived the whole scene. I was a bad experience to be subjected to twice.

'. . . two things, the sight of him staring at us like that and the feeling of Oliver's stiff cock inside me. Then he did one of his "practical jokes": he had a water pistol in his pocket and he took it out and squirted it against his head. What he didn't know, was that at the same moment something else was squirting – Oliver had been just ready to go off when Trent opened the door, and he couldn't wait another second . . . so there they were, the water pistol and the cock, both going off together; only one of them was inside me, hitting me hot and deliciously. It was too much and I came too. Neither one of us moved an inch – we just pressed hard against each other – but inside something indescribable was happening. I never felt anything like it – big throbs that shook me and kept coming . . . I guess it was because Trent was there looking at me getting laid like that . . . I don't even remember him going out and closing the door, I was much, much too . . .'

Trent stopped reading. It was too acutely painful a sensation. He felt weak: it was as if all the strength had been sapped out of him by the little book with the lavender cover. He felt vaguely that he should 'do something' – go into a rage, smash somebody with his fists –

but he couldn't move. He didn't have the force to get angry; he didn't even have the strength to stand up.

He sat numbly and, in spite of himself, brooded on the full scope of his misery. He had thought that the incident involving Vivian and Oliver was an isolated and meaningless episode, that it wasn't even entirely deplorable since it gave him the pretext to take a revenge which he assumed would be of more importance than the offense itself. He marveled now that he had been able to take it so casually when he had caught them in bed together, but it had been because he was so sure that he knew Vivian's character: he'd been so certain that she was incapable of indulging in sex for its own sake that he simply hadn't taken it seriously when he'd found her with Oliver. But now, this whole structure, which had formed the basis for his confidence, had crumbled, and in its place was the festering image of a Vivian so evil and treacherous that his mind could not find the limits of the disaster.

He could think of nothing to do. Mechanically, he began to read the awful book again.

'. . . told him anything that came into my head – that Oliver had taken advantage of me, that I was "alone" too much. I even told him it was *his* fault . . . I can't even remember all the things I told him. I cried a little too – that did it. He can't stand to see me cry. If he knew how easy it was . . .

'Then he wanted to make love naturally, wanted to favor me with one of those disgusting two-minute jobs of his when he gets on me all trembling with excitement and starts coming as soon as he gets in me . . . No thanks, I told him. Of course I had to let him paw my ass and my pussy for a little while – that was his "reward" for being a good boy and not having a scene.

'It's really funny how cold he leaves me. Any man in

139

the world excites me except *him*. Just sitting in a bus opposite some fat laborer and I can't keep myself from looking at the bulge his testicles make in his soiled working pants. And I don't care if he sees me looking . . . I even want him to, so he'll get the idea, so he'll know it's all right to say something and all right to get off the bus and take me to some filthy little hotel – any place, it doesn't matter so long as there's a bed and a door that locks . . .

'I love to do that – to get picked up by a stranger in a bus, on the street, anywhere. These are the dirtiest times, when I'm with a man I don't know at all; someone I've seen for the first time just a few minutes before . . . and then suddenly we're alone in a room . . . I can do anything then, the 69, let them do it to me in the behind – anything. When I made it with that French soldier I never even looked at his face at all – I love that, to just see their cocks and not even know what their faces are like. Right after I've just left Trent, that's when I feel most like doing it. The first man I see afterwards can always have me . . . It gets me so hot, that idea, to leave Trent and then to make love right away. Sometimes it's happened in a question of minutes, like that time with the cab driver after Trent got out at his school . . . I could see he was looking at me in the mirror. He could see my legs, too, so I opened them and let him really see something. He was so shy too – I could see the back of his neck get all red. I love that, to do things to shy men, especially young ones like the cab driver. I practically had to rape him. He got the idea finally though. I got up front with him after a while and we spent the whole afternoon driving around Paris – it's amazing what you can do in a moving car. He certainly didn't have many fares that day . . . God he was cute . . . he almost fainted when I put my head down in

140

his lap and began to lick his lollypop . . . and I kept kissing him in the ear, and whispering the dirtiest things I could think of, just to make him blush because he looked so pretty when he did it. We ended up driving right out of Paris and we found a lonely little road finally and stopped. I had to do everything; I even had to take his pants down. What a little doll he was! He didn't want to do it either because he'd just gotten married a week before. It was exquisite! I made him go down on me too. He'd never done that before. He was actually ashamed to look me in the face afterwards . . .'

Trent was blushing too, reading this, and his hands were trembling; most humiliating of all he'd been unable to prevent himself from being aroused by Vivian's lurid account of their private life, and as a result, had an insistent erection to contend with in the midst of his agony.

The book was a sort of poison, he knew. The more he read the worse he felt and he had no idea what he was going to do when he finished. It had occurred to him, after reading the first passage, that he might close the book and go over to Oliver's house and kill him – it seemed like one of the few things he might do that would give him some relief – but now he saw that there was also the French soldier and the fat laborer and the cab driver, and he'd only read a few pages. There were many more . . .

'. . . and I was having the most marvelous dream when the idiot came home and woke me up. There was something about a man dressed in animal skins who held one of my feet in one hand and kept rubbing and squeezing my pussy with the other. There was nothing I could do to stop him . . . it was enchanting; and there was something

141

about five young sailors, all kneeling around me and rubbing their cocks in my face. I was giving head to all of them and jacking them off . . . I can still remember what it felt like to have all those cocks at once . . . I could have killed him for waking me up. I was so hot that I sent him out of the room to make me a cup of tea so that I could play with myself a little. When he came back, I got him to take my "temperature" and made him move the thermometer back and forth slowly . . . He'd do anything I asked him. I actually think he likes things like that – he's the lowliest. It was delicious, playing with my clitoris and making him move that thermometer back and forth in my behind – I came just as he took it out. He was in seventh heaven just because I was letting him see my bottom – I should have made him kiss it, only that would have been too good for him! Anyway, he didn't know what was going on in the front . . . My whole life is like that – a perpetual orgasm taking place under his nose and he doesn't know! . . .'

Trent could see that he compulsively was going to read every word in the book despite the fact that it was torture to do so. He tried to prove to himself that this was not the case by forcing himself to get up from the table and walk away.

At first, this display of volition made him feel a little better, but after a few minutes of staring out the window and wondering what he would do when Vivian came home he began to feel worse than ever.

The flat was on the fourth floor and he got a very vivid prevision of what the next few seconds would be like were he to open the window, step on the sill and jump. He felt himself already in the air, falling so swiftly and with just the time to think, 'that was stupid.' He got frightened and tried to think of something else. Immediately he thought of Vivian and imagined what she might be doing at that moment; then he thought of the window again; then he went back to the table and re-opened the book.

'. . . love. I didn't think it was ever going to happen to me again, but I am; completely, idiotically, like a 16-year-old with a man who's just shown her for the first time what a delicious thing the male body is, and what heavenly things it can do!

'Maybe that's why I've fallen so hard for him – because he makes me feel so terribly young. The way I met him too . . . just the sort of situation in which a schoolgirl gets a crush on a boy – he "rescued" me. We'd gone to the Art Students' Ball and some drunken idiot was trying to tear my clothes off. He'd already pulled my halter off and was about to rip off the skirt and anything else he fancied . . . Trent, of course, was nowhere to be seen – he always manages to be some place else when a situation comes up which might involve a fight – I was in a completely ridiculous position; trying to hide my breasts with my hands; not seeing any way to stop him from stripping me nude. I didn't think anyone would help me because that sort of things always happens at affairs of that kind. I was very close to begin blubbering like a baby . . . and then there he was, tall, and wearing a leopard skin, and very, very cool. He said to give back my halter – not loudly or anything, but with a hell of a lot of danger in his voice . . . and he has a body like Perseus. The man didn't argue, gave me the halter at once and cleared out. Then he asked me to dance. That's how it started . . .

'He danced beautifully and, at first, discreetly, not touching me with anything but his hand on my back, and lightly at that. We were about the only couple who weren't making love while they danced. I asked him what he was and he said "Ashanti." That's the name of his tribe but I'd meant what kind of a costume was he wearing. Then he said, "Ah'm a *lehpid* man." I wanted to kiss him he said it so adorably, but my God he was handsome with his white plumes and his dark, lean body and his bracelets!

'Little by little, he began to dance more intimately. He did it as if it wasn't so much his idea as that he was simply following the music. It was a mambo, and he began to press me against him a little after the breaks and to put his thigh between my legs when we turned. I let him, it was what I wanted – to rub myself like a hot rabbit against his hardness and to have him move those big hands of his all over me . . . and there were other hands, lots of them, that fondled my buttocks and went into that grass skirt of Margot's that I was wearing to feel my legs and in between them . . .

'The music got more frantic and I began to wiggle my hips and my backside . . . I wanted him to dance with me the way African men know . . . there was just a lone saxophone, blowing low and very slowly and he put his hands on my rump and pumped me gently, letting me feel his thing – it was gigantic. I put my arms around his neck and strained my breasts against him. He put his knee between mine and forced me to open my legs and then, for about ten seconds, we stood there and fucked each other . . .

'When the music stopped I was panting and felt like I was on fire. He asked me what my name was and I said the first thing that came into my head: "Nicole." Then he asked me if I'd come and visit him the next afternoon and told me his address. I laughed in his face as if the proposition were so ludicrous that it wasn't even worth taking offense at, and I pretended I'd been making fun of him by dancing with him the way I had; then I walked off and left him without bothering to say goodbye. But that address of his was branded on my mind like the title of a book I was dying to read, and at 5 P.M. the next afternoon I was knocking at his door.

'I acted as if there weren't the slightest chance that anything was going to happen, and gave him to understand that he disgusted me physically – the way I do with Trent – but he didn't react the way Trent does, he didn't cringe like a mongrel as if he wanted to kiss my feet; he grinned at me and asked me if it wouldn't be all right if he just "licked my white pussy a tiny bit". It made me catch my breath, the way he said it. I told him my husband was a very important man in the government and asked him if he knew what could happen to him for saying such a thing to me; and I told him I thought he was a revolting ape and that he wasn't going to put his big paws on me . . . I was sitting in an armchair and he came toward me . . . I said, "Get away from me, you filthy nigger!" And then I got what I wanted so terribly much that I hadn't been able to sleep thinking about it – two stinging slaps in the face from a man that was about to take his pleasure of me exactly when and how he pleased . . . I shut my eyes in ecstasy and he knelt down and draped my legs over his shoulders and buried his face in my crotch . . . Even if I'd wanted to, I'd have been afraid to try and stop him after those vicious slaps.

'He caught the material of my panties in his teeth and tore them away with one twist of that neck of his . . .'

Trent read the book with mixed horror and pleasure. On the one hand, imagining the scene that Vivian was describing was physically painful to him, and on the other hand, he'd gotten so lecherous from imagining it that he *wanted* the most depraved orgy conceivable to occur and to be recounted in detail. In addition to these confused feelings he was disturbed still further by the ironical fact that here, before his eyes, was an example of spontaneous, and effective erotic writing – the very thing that he himself had been trying to do for weeks without success.

With the sweat glistening on his forehead, he perused what followed slowly and carefully, seeing each ruining word separately as it came drifting up from the page and exploded in his brain.

'. . . spread my legs and, with the tip of his tongue, teased my pussy exactly the way he said he would. It drove me out of my mind . . . I remember I was cursing and saying every terrible thing that came into my mind . . . I pulled my skirt above my ass and tried to screw his mouth . . . and then, when he saw I was on the verge of coming, he stopped, and stood up and laughed at me. I cursed and begged and pleaded with him to go on – I don't know what I said – and he calmly took off his trousers and went and lay down on the bed, making himself comfortable. He has the biggest, longest cock I ever saw in my life and he lay there grinning at me, not saying a word, and pointed to it with his finger. I ran across to him and started to mount him so that he could screw me, but that wasn't what he wanted and he grabbed me by the hair, making me turn around on him so that I was facing that colossal penis . . . then he forced my head down . . . closer and closer . . . I did what he wanted, and as soon as my lips touched it, I felt his tongue go flickering at my clitoris again, and his big lips press against my pussy . . .

'We did it that way and after we'd both reached our climax, *then* he rolled me over and began to screw me. It

146

went on all afternoon. I don't know how many times I came. I lost count. I felt like something was cooking in me and every little while it boiled over and ran down the sides of the pot. He can make love as long, and as many times as he wants. I didn't know there was a man like that . . . when he finally stopped, he went and got my pocket-book and opened it. There were two ten-thousand franc bills in it and he gave me a little smile and folded them and put them in his dresser drawer. He's magnificent. His name is Zila and I'm so much in love with him I don't know what to do. I'm hung up on those big, black eyes of his, and the way he walks, and the way he cuffs me in the face whenever I do something wrong, and, most of all, on that great brute of a hardon that he has permanently. I can't stand not being with him – I asked him today if he'd take me away with him and I think he will. I've got to get the money from the bank tomorrow. He wants to go to South America, he says, and if I get the plane tickets he'll leave with me. That way I'll be sure to have him for the next few weeks anyhow – I can't see any further than that, but that's enough. I never wanted anything so badly in my life. Oh Zila, Zila, Zila! . . . I love you!

'In the meantime, every moment I spend with Trent is unbearable. At night, when he touches me, it makes me sick to my stomach, and when I think of that sickly white penis of his – his hardon, to me, is like a shit, coming out of his body a little bit in front of where it should, but just that, a shit, a stinking turd that . . .'

Trent's mind went white. In the past few minutes he'd felt as if something in him like an elastic band had been seized by powerful hands and stretched to its utter limits. There was the point at which it could stretch no longer – he felt like that for all of five seconds and opened his mouth to shriek because it was as if all the marrow were being sucked out of his bones, and as if the live nerves were being pulled out of him in an excruciating, long thread – then it snapped and he leaped up from the table and rushed to the bathroom . . .

He yanked open the door to the medicine chest. It was full of tubes, bottles, boxes and cans, containing all the pills and unused medicines that had been accumulated since they'd been living in the flat. He grabbed a silver tube at random, glanced at the label: SYMPATHYL, and emptied it into his hand. Three oval, white pills rolled out. He popped them into his mouth and washed them down with a gulp of water from the faucet. Then he went back to the medicine chest. Moving at top speed, he began, systematically, to open every one of the various containers and to bolt, or pour the contents of each down his throat – EKTOGAN, TONEDRON, ADIAZINE, TENSOL, ORTHO-GASTRINE, EPHYNAL, LAR-GACTYL, ULTRAVITAMINE, VERMIFUGE, ANIO-DOL INTERNE, NEUROCALCIUM, GLUCO CALCIUM, CEQUINYL, DOCEMINE, CORAMINE-GLUCOSE, UROFORMINE, TESTOSTERONE: they all littered the floor, empty. He hadn't the slightest idea what they were – French medicines, each with its explanatory label telling the ingredients and recommended dosage. He ignored everything and swallowed it all, including nosedrops and suppositories. Then he staggered into the bedroom and fell on the floor.

11

When Trent had jerked open the medicine-chest door and devoured its contents, it had been mid-afternoon of a gray November day. For the next few hours his still body lay where it had fallen and the only thing that occurred in the absolutely silent apartment was that the rooms grew darker and darker as the daylight waned.

Finally the pale day, which like so many others of the Paris autumn was hardly to be called a day at all, but rather a long twilight, lapsed into the darkness it had so imperfectly separated from. Outside, the street lights went on and the customary bustle of people returning home from work began. In the apartment, the deathly silence continued; then, a little after six P.M., there was the sound of a key turning in the lock; the door opened, a hand reached in and snapped on the hall light and Vivian appeared.

Immediately on entering, she kicked off her high-heel pumps, then, taking a pair of slippers from a closet in the hall, she put them on and sighed with pleasure. Next, she took off her coat and a minute, blue hat she was wearing, put them in the closet and, fluffing at her blonde hair, headed for the mirror in the bathroom.

She put on the light and saw the strange assemblage of empty medicine bottles and boxes. After looking at it blankly for several moments she knelt and, one by one, tossed the various containers into a wastebasket; then she got back to the graver business of inspecting her face in the mirror and doing some necessary repair work after the trials and fatigues of her day. This entailed the use of tweezers, creams, brushes, pencils, salves, ointments, clippers, combs, atomizers, tissues, depilatories, lotions, powders, pomades, pins, pastes, perfumes and puffs, and took thirty-five minutes.

Feeling fresh and restored, she took a basin from the bathroom and went to the living room where she opened a drawer of the secretary and took out a bottle of tincture of ipecacuanha (fortunately, this emetic was where it was, since, if it had been in the medicine chest, Trent would have gobbled it up with the rest). Then, she went to the bedroom.

Vivian turned on the table lamp and looked intently at her husband's prostrate form. Trent's face was an ashen gray and he didn't seem to be breathing. Nevertheless, Vivian didn't appear to be alarmed or even surprised. She propped him up in a sitting position and went and opened the window so that the fresh air blew in on his face. Then she left the room and returned after a few moments with a wet sponge and a bottle of smelling salts.

After a quarter hour of being sponged, slapped in the face and having the smelling salts passed beneath his nostrils, Trent miraculously began to show signs of life: certain muscles in his face began to twitch; his chest rose and fell in feeble respiration and he started to groan faintly. Vivian then administered the ipecac and waited holding the basin. Soon he vomited – with much violence and for a long time. When he was done, she maneuvered him on to the bed where she took off all his clothes except his underwear, and put him under the covers.

By this time, Trent had recovered consciousness and lay staring at her, weak and terrified.

'Why are you looking at me like that?' Vivian asked, drawing a chair up to the bedside and sitting down.

150

Trent's lips trembled but no words came out. Two large tears formed in his eyes.

Vivian said matter of factly: 'If you're afraid I'm going to murder you or something, you can stop worrying.'

'Wh-wh-why?'

'Because I love you, you silly old bastard.' She leaned forward and tucked in a dangling corner of the sheet.

Both tears fell out of Trent's eyes and were replaced by two new ones. 'Why?' he said again.

'Why do I love you?' Vivian wasn't sure what the 'why' referred to. Trent wasn't either. It meant: 'Why did this happen?' 'Why did you do what you did?' 'Why are you being so nice now? . . .'

He looked at her through the watery film of his tears – voluptuous; her breasts, her lips, her thighs and legs all slightly fuller than with other women, and yet her hands and the features of her face were fashioned with extraordinary fineness and delicacy. She was a Venus-like woman, not a slim, terribly young adolescent like Margot, new to her beauty, new to life, but a woman; full-formed and at the height of her ripe, feminine loveliness; a woman who knew what the earthly pleasures were and how to enjoy them. 'Yes,' he said. 'Why do you love me?'

'You're the only man I could ever stand to be with.'

Something must have gone wrong with Zila, Trent thought immediately, this must be the rebound. 'Listen, you don't have to say things like that . . . I saw your journal: I've been reading it all afternoon.'

'I know.'

'Well, according to your journal, I'm the only man you *can't* stand to be with.'

'The journal isn't true,' Vivian stated.

Trent raised his eyebrows, knocking one of the remaining tears out of his eyes.

'It's not true, that's all. I wanted you to see it. I even gave the old lady 200 francs to bring my pocketbook and say she found it in the park.'

'But why?'

'I wanted to see if you were in love with Margot.'

'Margot?'

'Well, you don't have to sound so goddamn surprised about it, you have a journal too, you know, and yours *was* a secret one – it wasn't supposed to be seen by me at all.'

Trent sat up in the bed with a start. 'What are you talking about?'

'I'm talking about you, Mr Monkeybar, and the gym of the American Club and Sunday morning and . . .'

'That was my notebook! How could you be reading that?'

'I happened to be going through your pockets one night, as I often do, and there it was. You certainly weren't very careful with it.'

'But you don't actually think – '

Vivian did. She gave him a hard look which proved it. Trent opened his mouth and laughed silently. 'I don't think it's so very funny,' she observed. 'I understand that I had it coming to me – after what I did with Oliver – but for some strange reason I fail to see why it's something to get hilarious about . . .'

'Listen, it's very funny. That thing that you read didn't really happen – it was a chapter, a passage from a book . . . I didn't tell you, but I've been working on a novel, and that story about Margot and the American Club is part of it.'

Vivian's eyes widened and she said: '*You're* writing a book?'

'I haven't written too much of it yet – just that part that

152

you read, as a matter of fact – but I've got lots of notes and outlines, and I'm just about ready to start writing for real.'

This time it was Vivian's turn to laugh. 'What is it?' Trent asked, getting a trifle annoyed.

'I've got a surprise for you,' she giggled delightedly. 'I'm writing a book too – it's done for that matter. That's where those things came from that you read in what you thought was my "secret journal" – I just copied them out of the manuscript. What's more, it's going to be published! . . . by the same man that publishes Margot's books. . .'

'Ben?' Trent asked in astonishment.

'Yes. Why, do you know him? Margot introduced me to him because it was her idea that I write the book in the first place – she told me it would be a good idea to write something that would make it look as if I were a terrible bitch; frigid with my husband and a nymphomaniac with everybody else.'

'I suppose she told you that you ought to "experience personally" the things you were writing about.'

'That's right! How'd you know? "Learn your heroine" she kept saying. She said I ought to go to any lengths to see what it would feel like if I were a character in my own book. That's the real reason why I went to bed with Oliver – I was playing at being a scarlet woman.'

Trent couldn't help remembering her written description of this scene and how painful it had been for him. 'That's one part of your journal that you couldn't say wasn't true,' he reminded her.

'It's the only part,' Vivian claimed stoutly, 'and the things I say about it are completely untrue.'

'What about Zila? You didn't invent him; I saw him,

153

with his ostrich feathers and his "gigantic thing," and what about that thermometer story. That – '

'He was very nice, he got me out of a very embarrassing situation and I danced with him. He danced very properly and he never said a word to me. Everything else I wrote about him I made up, including his name; but while we're on the subject of the dance, what about you, dancing with Margot like a sex-starved orangutan? And dashing off down the hall with that Egyptian whore?'

He was getting into hot water and he decided he'd better drop the whole thing.

'. . . that was quite an exhibition you put on that night,' Vivian was saying, 'and when I saw what you wrote about raping Margot, I began to see that there was really something going on between you two. That's when I decided I wanted you to accidently stumble on my "journal." You're such a connoisseur of practical jokes, I thought it was about time that the cigar blew up in *your* face. Most of all, I wanted to see what you'd do – I knew that if you really were hung up on Margot it wouldn't make any difference to you . . .'

What she said made sense. He saw all at once that her horrifying journal had indeed been designed for him and that, even though her pride didn't let her admit it, it testified to her jealousy. After all, the very fact of her writing a journal at all was her angry response to the one of his that she'd read; and then her account of meeting Zila at the ball and what followed – wasn't that to get back at him, for the way he had behaved that night?

This discovery made him feel excellent. He realized that even though he would always wonder if there weren't more truth in her 'journal' than she admitted to; that whether her alibi were true, or just what she wanted him to think, the mere fact that it was so important to her for

154

him to believe it was inconsistent with the monstrous image he'd had of her, and refuted it. It was then that he previewed that they might live happily – sexually, that is – ever after.

'That must be quite a book you wrote,' he said, 'it almost killed me, what I read of it. Have you got it here? I'd like to see it. And what's the title?'

'*Sin for Breakfast*,' Vivian said getting up and going out of the room. He could hear her rummaging in a closet.

'That's a very good title,' he called out.

Vivian came back with a thick, typewritten manuscript and handed it to him.

'By the way,' Trent observed, taking it and hefting it wistfully, 'I hope you're not thinking of using your right name as the author – that would be charming if my mother or somebody ran across the book and saw it was by you . . .'

'Naturally. I'm not completely out of my mind, you know. I've thought of a few names . . . I think it's going to be "Hamilton Drake".'

'"Hamilton Drake?" That stinks. That's no kind of a name for the author of a book like that. What you want is something latin and exotic . . . something like "Akbar del Piombo", or "Faustino Perez". They really sound like spicy writers. "Hamilton Drake" sounds like a theological student.'

'Oh, I don't think it's as bad as all that – '

'It *is*,' Trent snapped. 'As a matter of fact, I won't allow it . . . Why, a thing like that is enough to spoil the book's chances of being read by a lot of people. I *insist* that you find another name. Do you hear me? . . . I'm your husband and . . .'

'All right, we'll talk about it another time,' Vivian said quietly.

Trent turned his attention to the manuscript he was holding. He turned to the first page and read the opening sentences which went:

'If anyone in the café thought it odd that he had been sitting for over half an hour without shifting his gaze from the house across the street, he hardly cared. There was a magnificent view of Oliver's door and . . .'

He leafed through the pages rapidly, stopping once in a while to read short passages. When he'd almost gotten to the end and had just read the long list of medicines which he'd wolfed down in his attempted suicide, he said: 'I'm glad that happened in a book – if I'd ever swallowed all that mess in real life it probably would have killed me.'

Then he turned to the end of the story and read the final pages, which were as follows:

'Vivian gave him a peculiar look and got to her feet. Her eyes not leaving his, her hands moved to her side and slowly unzipped her skirt. She wriggled out of it and it dropped to her feet. She kicked it contemptuously into a corner of the room and, crossing her arms, swiftly yanked her sweater over her head and flung it after the skirt. When her face came out of the sweater the eyes were still staring in his own. She reached beneath the slip now, did something, and suddenly her stockings, her garter belt, and her panties all lay in a pile on the floor. Then came the slip, slowly, exposing all the contours of her breath-taking nudity as it mounted – her legs; her sleek thighs; the tawny bush between them; her round, soft belly (she wore no brassiere and the reason now became apparent), the full, pink-tipped breasts, straining outward and jig-gling at her slightest movement as if they were on springs. The slip too was tossed on the floor – she looked like a man getting ready for a fight.

'She was standing inches away from him and she was

naked! He'd never seen her bare like this and so close! She reached, and with a violent tug, stripped the sheet and covers off him. He was sitting up in the bed in his shorts and undershirt, feeling weak and ridiculous, and when she vigorously pushed him he went over sideways like a sack of something soft.

'In an instant she was on him – covering him, rolling on him, smothering him with her hot thighs and breasts; and with her mouth, biting, kissing, licking – annihilating him. She was a tigress, mouthing him in a frenzy of starvation, rapaciously spoiling him . . .

'In the course of the next few minutes, his underwear came off of its own accord and he lay trapped beneath her like a bare, helpless lamb.

'She straddled him, and he felt the hard points of her breasts as she leaned and rubbed her half-open mouth against his. The full lips and ardent tongue browsed ceaselessly and, at the same time, he felt her hand tickling his testicles. It sent a nervous shudder of pleasure through his body and stiffened his cock to a degree that was almost painful . . .

'She took hold it it now, in her fist, and rubbed it gently against her sex, caressing her clitoris with the silk-smooth skin of the knob . . .

'"Oh Jesus," she moaned, "that feels so fucking good!"

'Then she directed the hard truncheon in her hand a little further down to the hot and avid hole where it belonged. Trent's erection was so huge that it seemed at first that it wouldn't be able to enter this nether-mouth of hers, as much as it stretched and strained to swallow the visitor. But Vivian maneuvered expertly, shifting her body till she found the ideal angle of ingress, and first the tip – then slowly the head, and all the inches of Trent's hardon worked their way into the dark, moist paradise

. . . then slowly, it debouched again – out, out, out until it was almost free before it began the counter-stroke . . . a little faster this time, as her vagina finally took the measure of the fleshy piston in her . . .

'Soon it was sliding freely in and out – drawing out for almost its entire length, then plunging deeply back and striking the extreme back limit of her sheath so that she groaned with delight.

'Trent noted amazedly that even though they had been copulating in the most licentious fashion for several minutes, that he was still in good control of himself. Ordinarily, he would have had his spasm in the opening seconds of the encounter. Taking confidence from this unprecedented power, he grasped her firmly by the buttocks and began to screw her with a will. Up to now, it had been Vivian who had been rising and sinking on him and he had lain more or less passively, blissfully allowing himself to be raped; but, at present, it was he who, squeezing her rump, forced her down and thrust up to meet her. And soon, holding her tightly pressed against him, he swung her down and rolled over, coming up on top of her without having withdrawn.

'Now he dominated her, looming above and plowing her like a master. He allowed his cock to come out entirely and bumped it soft and teasingly against her gaping pussy – again and again until she began to sob with the yearning she had to have it back inside . . . Then, he lunged with all his weight speeding his pole into her slit to the hilt and making her gasp with ecstasy.

'He felt perfectly confident that he would be able to keep on as long as was necessary to bring her to the climax and that only then would he allow himself to finish in his turn. He reasoned that this unheard of virility of his must have come as a result of one of the medicines he'd taken, or from the combination of all of them, and it even flashed through his mind that he might have to repeat the fantastic dose whenever he was going to make love with her. He didn't realize that the medicines had nothing to do with the matter; that his new-found capabilities were a reaction to the fact that, for the first time, Vivian was acting as if she wanted to screw, wanted *him* to screw her . . .

'He went on with his game – withdrawing completely and then touching her gently, and repeatedly, with the tip of his rod while she squirmed below in an agony of desire and begged him to put it back . . . and suddenly lancing into her and poking and wiggling and screwing for several wild minutes before extracting himself.

'There came a time when she was so close to having her orgasm, during one of these periods of delirious pitching and squirming, that she scratched his buttocks like a wildcat and tried with all her strength to prevent him from drawing his penis out the way he had been doing. But he persisted and left her for five whole seconds, poised on the very brink of the great nervous reflex that her soul and body demanded . . . Then he stabbed; and Vivian, overwhelmed, convulsed and shook as throb after throb of rapture pulsed from her cunt and surged through her, streaking her mind with ecstasy and tingling the tips of her toes; and Trent too, with supreme satisfaction, released his pent-up passion and came in her.'

Trent placed the last page carefully on the pile and put the manuscript on the bed beside him. He could think of nothing to say and sat silently, not daring to look at her. Even after reading this vivid sketch, he still found it incredible to think that Vivian might actually desire him. He was still smarting from the terrible insults he'd received in her 'journal.' And there were all the incidents

159

of the past; all the times she'd rejected him unmercifully and made no effort to conceal that he disgusted her . . .

Could it really be possible that, shocked at the thought that he and Margot had been having an affair, she had been so extremely jealous, had changed so completely?

'I just can't believe that you actually feel this way,' he blubbered. 'I – '

Vivan gave him a peculiar look and got to her feet . . .